THE SHIP OF SWALLOWS

EDWARD THOMAS

The Ship of Swallows

A selection of short stories
edited and introduced by
JEREMY HOOKER

Preface by
MYFANWY THOMAS

ENITHARMON PRESS

First published in 2005
by Enitharmon Press
26B Caversham Road
London NW5 2DU

www.enitharmon.co.uk

Distributed in the UK by
Central Books
99 Wallis Road
London E9 5LN

Distributed in the USA and Canada
by Dufour Editions Inc.
PO Box 7, Chester Springs
PA 19425, USA

Introduction © Jeremy Hooker 2005
Preface © Myfanwy Thomas 2005

ISBN 1 904634 16 8 (hardback)
ISBN 1 904634 25 7 (signed edition, limited
to 35 copies slipcased by The Fine Bindery)

Enitharmon Press gratefully acknowledges the financial support of
Arts Council England, London.

British Library Cataloguing-in-Publication Data.
A catalogue record for this book is available
from the British Library.

Typeset in Caslon 540 by Servis Filmsetting Ltd
and printed in England by
Antony Rowe Ltd

Contents

Preface by Myfanwy Thomas   7
Introduction by Jeremy Hooker   9

*

The First of Spring	15
Sunday Afternoon	26
Milking	35
The Flower-Gatherer	39
Home	43
Hawthornden	52
The Artist	57
The Attempt	61
Morgan	67
The Ship of Swallows	75
A Third-Class Carriage	78
The Pilgrim	81
The Friend of the Blackbird	85
The Land of Youth	90
The Making of the Worlds, of Gods, and of Giants	98
One Swallow Doesn't Make a Summer	104
Birds of a Feather Flock Together	106

ACKNOWLEDGEMENTS

The stories have been drawn from the following books:

'The First of Spring', 'Sunday Afternoon', and 'Milking' from *Rest and Unrest* (Duckworth, 1910); 'The Flower-Gatherer', 'Home', 'Hawthornden', 'The Artist', and 'The Attempt' from *Light and Twilight* (Duckworth, 1911); 'Morgan' and 'The Ship of Swallows' from *Cloud Castle and other papers* (Duckworth, 1922); 'A Third-Class Carriage', 'The Pilgrim', and 'The Friend of the Blackbird' from *The Last Sheaf: Essays by Edward Thomas* (Jonathan Cape, 1928); 'The Land of Youth' from *Celtic Stories* (The Clarendon Press, 1911); 'The Making of the Worlds, of Gods, and of Giants' from *Norse Tales* (The Clarendon Press, 1912); 'One Swallow Doesn't Make a Summer' and 'Birds of a Feather Flock Together' from *Four-and-Twenty Blackbirds* (Duckworth, 1915).

The publisher wishes to thank Richard Emeny of the Edward Thomas Fellowship for lending an unpublished photograph of Edward Thomas to reproduce on the book-jacket. The photograph, from the collection of Myfanwy Thomas, was taken in Swindon *c.* 1902.

The frontispiece shows Edward Thomas at Steep, Hampshire, midsummer 1914 (photograph reproduced by kind permission of Cardiff University Library, Edward Thomas Archive © Cardiff University).

Preface

Oddly enough, as far as I remember, my father never read his own stories and poems aloud to his three children. By the time he had written *Four-and-Twenty Blackbirds* in 1915, Merfyn and Bronwen were in their mid-teens and I was five. But he did read aloud to us the enchanting *Three Mulla Mulgars* (now renamed *The Three Royal Monkeys)* by Walter de la Mare, having written enthusiastic reviews in at least three different journals. He also told me – not reading them – stories from the *Norse Tales*. I remember Three Billy Goats Gruff, the Trolls and other unfamiliar characters. He also sang to us sea shanties, folk songs and later songs he learned when he joined the Artists' Rifles.

He never 'talked down' to children and they responded to his understanding. A conventionally brought-up London cousin, Margaret, between the ages of my brother and sister, often stayed with us in the holidays. She found the two older children too boisterous and was lonely. My father saw that she was disconsolate and they went for a walk, when she learned about the birds and wildflowers: Margaret never forgot his slightly aloof kindness.

I remember Mother telling me that when five-year-old Merfyn, on his father's knee, listening to a ballad he was reading aloud, heard the word 'victor' come into it, he said solemnly, 'I know a boy called Victor.' I noticed when reading one of the stories in this book, he had used this incident in a slightly different context.

My father also used in a story here, and in a poem, a vivid description of the swift's flight – 'as though the bow had flown off the arrow' – which he first heard from one of Robert Frost's daughters. He first asked her permission to use it!

Several of the pieces here are keenly described incidents, almost dreamlike. Those that I have read for the first time I greatly enjoyed. Such a variety and detailed observation of scenes in them! Many of the characters, as Jeremy Hooker points out, are variations of the author's own self-consciousness or lack of confidence – but always interesting. I am delighted that they have been brought together in this collection.

MYFANWY THOMAS

Dedicated to the
memory of
Myfanwy Thomas
16 August 1910 – 8 March 2005

INTRODUCTION

In September 1905 Edward Thomas wrote to Gordon Bottomley: 'I see that I may come to stories of some kind'. As late as May 1915, some six months after he had begun to write poetry, he wrote to Robert Frost: 'I suppose I ought to write a long short story about a man who didn't enlist'. The tone here is characteristically self-mocking at the expense of his indecisiveness, which was a joke between Thomas and Frost; but there is no reason to suppose Thomas was not still thinking of himself, at least potentially, as a writer of fiction.

The stories that he did actually write – published in *Rest and Unrest* (1910) and *Light and Twilight* (1911), in *Celtic Stories* (1911), *Norse Tales* (1912), his versions of English proverbs, *Four-and-Twenty Blackbirds* (1915), and in posthumous collections of his writings – were a creative outlet next in importance to his poetry for Thomas, and constitute a significant achievement in their own right. His strongest impulse to write fiction first occurred early in 1909. On 13 February that year he wrote to Bottomley: 'I have been writing not reviews, not commissioned books, not landscapes, but character sketches stories &c., . . . Since the beginning of the year I have had an extraordinary energy in writing . . .' What he then goes on to say shows why he returned from stories to reviews and commissioned books: 'Most are unfit for the papers & magazines by being too unpleasant, or too fanciful, or too quiet. So it seems to me I shall have an empty belly (I haven't earned anything yet this year). But I shall make up for that by a swelled head.'

Edward Thomas wrote stories, as he said, 'under a real impulse', but knew that he could not make a living by doing so. Irrespective of commercial considerations, however, his interest in storytelling was fundamental to his imaginative life as a whole. Not only is a narrative element important in his poetry, but, from the outset, fiction, in the form of myth, preoccupied him. In both *Oxford* (1903) and *Beautiful Wales* (1905) Thomas had shown his wish for 'a new mythology'. But what did 'myth' mean to him? More, certainly, than the weak dictionary definition of 'purely fictitious narrative'.

Thomas's interest in myth related to his need for a sense of connection, of belonging. In *In Pursuit of Spring* (1914) he wrote of 'the fact that the earth does not belong to man, but man to the earth'. This may be described as a function of myth in its most fundamental sense: a story about the proper relation of the human to the non-human world, a tale that reveals the truth about man's place on earth.

For most of his adult life, Thomas knew how far he was from living in accordance with this truth – it was the knowledge that distinguished his self-lacerating honesty. Born and brought up in the London suburbs, he was an incomer to the country, and an acute critic of the ideals and illusions to which people in his position were prone. As the artist in 'The Ship of Swallows' indignantly proclaims: 'This Nature poetry-stuff is the jejune enthusiasm of townsmen who are ashamed to confess that they are such'. Thomas explored the subject further in *The Country* (1913): 'only a rarefied conscious appreciation is made possible by detachment and the severing of all bonds of necessity'. At issue in this severing is the consequent inauthenticity of being and the false poetry that springs from it. This, in brief, is the explanation of why Thomas could only realize himself as a poet by establishing bonds of necessity – with the earth, with England, in wartime.

Thomas diagnosed his own condition unsparingly, and, as he showed in writing to Eleanor Farjeon, his analytic self-understanding was part of the problem: 'You see the central evil is self-consciousness carried as far beyond selfishness as selfishness is beyond self denial, (not very scientific comparison) and now amounting to a disease and all I have got to fight it with is the knowledge that in truth I am not the isolated selfconsidering brain which I have come to seem.' The torments of self-consciousness are a recurrent theme in Thomas's stories and poems, as are the means of escape – childhood and death.

His preoccupation with childhood is frequently associated, in one form or under one image or another, with the myth of earthly Paradise, of what in 'Home' he calls 'That land, / My home, I have never seen'. This, in turn, is associated with his Welshness, and his hiraeth for Wales. In *The South Country* (1909) he wrote: 'As mankind has looked back to a golden age, so the individual, repeating the history of the race, looks back and finds one in his own past'. In 'The First of Spring' Alice Lacking remembers her eleven-year-old self, when 'She and her mother possessed the world'. Significantly, as Thomas's own bookishness infects some of his literary work with unreality, so it is books that have divorced Alice from this early self, when writing poetry contributed to fullness of being, and 'upon everything was a seal of everlastingness'. 'Home' is Thomas's most complete fictionalization of his identification of the fuller life with Wales. Here we see, too, that the desired enlargement of being is both spiritual and social, the country (unnamed, but, obviously, Wales) being, for the boy and his father, both 'the country of their souls' and where there is 'a kind of common life as of one big family'.

W. H. Hudson, commenting on Thomas's one novel *The Happy-Go-Lucky Morgans* (1913), remarked that all his fictional persons 'are one and all just Edward Thomas'. Hudson ascribed this phenomenon to Thomas being 'essentially a poet'. There is truth in Hudson's comment as far as Thomas's stories as well as the novel are concerned. It is one of the things that make the difference between the original stories and the retellings of traditional tales, which have a narrative drive largely lacking in the stories involving character analysis. It is also what helps to give the latter considerable psychological interest. A number of characters in the stories – for example, Morgan, Morgan Traheron, Hawthornden, both men in 'The Pilgrim' – are projections of Thomas himself, and the name 'Lacking' points unequivocally to the discontent that was Thomas's own. Hudson's judgment need not be as limiting as it sounds, however. For while the stories would be interesting for what they reveal of their author, their psychological penetration of a not uncommon malaise ensures that they have a wider interest, too.

The part played by 'poetry' and 'mysticism' in the stories is significant. In the version of 'Morgan' which appears as a chapter in *The Happy-Go-Lucky Morgans*, Morgan's mother says of her son: 'He writes quite seriously, as actors half seriously talk, in tones quite inhumanly sublime'. She describes him also as 'too poetical'. The latter, one feels, is what kept Thomas from poetry, until he learnt, partly from Robert Frost, to trust the poetry inherent in speech. In the stories the 'poetical' appears especially in evocations of nature, as in the personification of 'the lusty, buxom spring, a pretty and merry slut' at the beginning of 'Milking'. It may be contrasted with effective observation, as in the description of a blackcap singing in 'The Friend of the Blackbird': 'The little dead-leaf coloured bird quivered all over; his throat swelled in bubble after bubble; his lifted black head was turned from side to side as he sang; and he moved slowly among the blossom'. Theatrical sublimity, like the poetical, is an aspect of Thomas's ambivalent treatment of mysticism. He described Richard Jefferies, whom he greatly admired, as 'a mystic'. Writing about Maurice Maeterlinck, on the other hand, he said: 'The term "mystic" is not to be dwelt on too seriously, because it is now in an advanced stage of popular corruption.' The problem Thomas grapples with in 'Morgan' is that of attempting to express his character's genuinely mystical and social impulses while at the same time being aware of an unreality deriving from Morgan's severing of bonds of necessity. Hawthornden's 'dim-pinnacled citadel of unreality' expresses a similar malaise.

Thomas comes down to earth in his poetry with more confidence than he shows in most of his imaginative prose. His poem 'Wind and Mist' is virtually an allegory of Thomas's life, partly 'lived in the clouds', with 'mist / Like chaos surging back'. As the speaker says:

> 'I did not know it was the earth I loved
> Until I tried to live there in the clouds
> And the earth turned to cloud.'

That he drew upon his own experience even in his retelling of traditional stories can be seen in the similarity between this experience and Gangler's memory of a scene 'like Niflheim' in 'The Making of the Worlds, of Gods, and of Giants' in *Norse Tales*: 'His house and the little piece of ground where he was standing seemed to be all that was left of the earth. The night's storm had washed away all the rest, and there he was shipwrecked in a sea of clouds and mist'. The image of a robin singing in Iron Wood in the same tale is another instance of certain imagistic and thematic continuities between the stories and the poetry.

It is not only such instances, however, that give Edward Thomas's stories their interest. Nor is the fact that the stories may be seen as a preparatory stage on the way to the poetry. It would be foolish to claim that the stories can stand as works of art comparable to the work of writers such as D. H. Lawrence, James Joyce and Katherine Mansfield, who were shaping the modern short story in English in the opening decades of the twentieth century. Thomas's shaping imagination achieved its finest embodiment in his poetry. His stories, however, both reveal 'the real impulse' under which they were written, and represent Thomas's whole effort to shape imaginative responses to fundamental questions of life and death, the self, and reality. To know Thomas's achievement as a writer it is necessary to know the best of his stories as well as his poetry and criticism.

JEREMY HOOKER

The First of Spring

ALICE LACKING had reached an age when already one man had confided in her his admiration for one of her friends scarcely younger than herself, one of those friends who already called her a dear old thing. In comment she allowed herself one of those faintly twitching smiles which seems to most people exquisitely tender, resigned, and sweet. Though but thirty-one years old she was one of the goddesses of twilight, pensive – restful – dim; at least, she gave others rest. She was tall but stooped; her hair was black and noticeable only for its sharp edge against her pale face, which was bony and a little askew; her dark eyes were ardent, and constantly rebelling against the tired expression which her white eyelids tended to give by slipping down. She talked little, but most of all when younger women and much younger men chanced to speak to her of poetry. A young wife suddenly thoughtful, with one child and a hunting husband who drank, would come to her with Browning's 'Parting at Morning'; and Alice would look into her eyes . . . and explain . . . in a comforting way: the young wife would look back and press her child to her breast and give a glance of perhaps melancholy discontent that the unmarried Alice should be so wise and then lastly smile with faint self-approval, as much as to say, 'At least, she cannot know everything': and Alice would caress the child. Perhaps she gave such women a faint thirst for revenge, and their way was to remark, during a whole ten years, how extraordinary it was that no man had insisted on marrying her; it was taken for granted she would be fastidious, reluctant.

For a year Alice was seriously ill. She became so much paler and her smile so much more painful in its sweetness that everyone was sorry, albeit pitiful. She kept more to her bees now and talked less than ever. She walked alone as she had always liked to do. Every week she repeated the same three or four walks several times, often the same twice a day, though laughing at herself and vowing not to do so again. Wet or fine she walked, apparently with indifference, except that her eyes were brightest in rain; both soft and stinging rain made her sing. She looked forward to the spring as to a great certain good, enjoyed all its tortuous approaches and withdrawings, yes, every one, so that the healthy fortunate men and women who went about bluffly complaining that it was too cold or too warm or too windy or too wet had throughout February and March at least one consolation, that they could joke at the expense of Alice who professed to like each separate day and its ways; and after hearing the opinion from one clever man they all agreed that she must be a pessimist at heart, or she could never be so different from them all, plain fox-hunting or agricultural or do-nothing people, optimists, of course.

Spring really seemed to have come on the twenty-seventh of March as Alice stepped out of the house and saw, though it was only two hours after sunrise, the single yellow crocuses pressed flat by the kisses of the sun, and one broad cluster of the same flowers – that could not open so wide because their petals touched – glowing as brightly as if there, at the foot of the oldest oak, the marriage of sun and earth had been consummated and was now giving birth to a child as glorious as the sun himself and also lowly and meek as earth, the mother. Beyond the edge of the garden was the hollow vale of grey-green grass, and dark woods each slightly lifted up on a gentle hillock, and water shining between, and jackdaws playing half a mile high, so far away that they were no bigger than flies and sometimes invisible, and yet their joy as clear as if it were crying out in her brain. The vale was bounded by naked, undulating hills and, above them, sunny white haze and, above that, layers of rounded white cloud melting below into the haze and behind into the blue that was almost white.

The grass was not yet green, the woods were still dark, but that could not postpone the spring. The river shone in the vale, the white roads on the opposite hills; but that did not make the spring. She knew it was spring by a grey cart horse that went by straining at a load: three brass bells tinkled and glittered between his ears and three behind his neck; his brow carried a brass crescent and four others hung before his chest; and there were scarlet ribbons about his head. There was spring in the smoke lying in a hundred white vertebræ motionless behind the rapid locomotive in the vale. There was spring in the crowing of a cock, in the silence that followed, in the crunch of distant wheels on the drying road, in the voice of the horse whinnying in his dark stall, in the childish blue of the sky between the pure white flocks at the zenith. Two girls, Alice's neighbours, dark bold girls, with deep voices, who raced about the countryside, kept poultry and dressed with an untidiness which all ridiculed and envied, rushed by; one said, 'We're going to play tennis this afternoon, and let the lawn go hang,' and the other, 'Come and look at our March chickens': and in them also there was spring. But without these things there was a something in the landscape which made her forget that it had looked haggard yesterday, haggard and drenched, hardly consenting to live; a something in the mist of love faintly enveloping the vale, not to be heard, seen, touched, tasted or even smelt, that told her it was spring; and with this inner certainty she descended the hill from her gate almost without using eyes and ears.

The steep road was disused, dry as a bone, but lumpy and hard, its unbroken flints polished like iron. Alice went down faster than she wished, and half way down she paused, already hot and fatigued. The weather which filled her with a desire to do more than she had ever done before, left her at the same time as weak as a child and on the edge of inexplicable tears. She went in under the unfenced trees at the side of the road, and sat down upon a trunk that lay mossy among a thousand wide open yellow flowers of celandine. Through the trees she could see the valley again, spread out at the foot of the hill which the road descended. She looked at it without seeing it. She half-closed her eyes to keep out the dazzle of the celandines. Her flesh, her brain, her nature, was sopped in spring like bread in wine. Her shoulders drooped forward, her neck bent, her hands supported themselves on the fallen tree, her legs changed their position slowly as if arranging themselves for sleep. She seemed to be dissolving in the languid air, her mortal flesh quivering as it acknowledged the spiritual things. Two bright chaffinches fighting and chirrupping as they chased one another swiftly through the air took her breath away. Nothing could have been more intimately and exquisitely pleasant than the first moments as she sat down, if it had not been that something in her mind rebelled, was discontented, tremulous, unhappy, and that not on account of any thought left in it from the remote or immediate past, but only, as far as she knew, because along with the surrender to the deep, rich, calm flood of spring came again an aspiration as in former springs, a desire as deep as her nature, a strong but vague and wordless desire to be something other than she was, to do something other than she was doing or had ever done – an unsatisfied desire, a worship without a skilled priest, nay! without a god even.

The laugh of a woodpecker awakened her; in her mood it was as if the laugh was her own but none the less surprising; she rose and went on down the hill. The trees on the side away from the valley were dark as if winter hid there yet, but the hazels filled the dark air with yellow and orange catkins as with vibrating dancing flowers. Alice lifted a hand as if to catch one of the loosest and ripest of the catkins, but it hung high and her hand fell again to her side. She started to run, but her limbs were unwilling, and she blushed at the ungainly failure as if she might have been seen. She walked slowly, looking down at the road and shutting out all thought, remaining only just aware that but a feeble crust covered over and kept down the seething in her mind. Before reaching the bottom she again sat down and gazed over the oak tops of a little wood, waiting and not quite unconsciously expecting that covering crust to break, perhaps helping herself to break it. And as she sat motionless the notes of a travelling organ, played in the garden of one of the houses hidden behind the oaks, rose up to her ears. It was a too slowly played tune, heavy to sickness with insincere emotion. Unembodied, uncontrolled by any passion or personality in the composer or the performer, the notes were floating about the world in a loose haze that might presently fade altogether, or on the other hand take some human shape by entering a human ear. Alice frowned and yet at the same time gave to the music just that shape which it desired in order to live and work its proper enchantment. It entered her spirit and she heard the organ with her ears no longer. The old Italian with one hand in his pocket and the other on the organ handle was playing one tune in the far-off garden, a different one in Alice.

To the sound of that music was painted and sung and spoken a tale beginning when she was eleven.

She saw herself a bright-cheeked girl, even then too thin, her eyes much larger than now, with a mane of heavy curling hair clipped short at her shoulders because it was too heavy. She wore a dress of green and yellow, as green and yellow as a furze bush that is half flowers. She was sitting curled up in a big arm-chair by an open window. It was June and not yet dawn, and all the house was asleep except the Irish terrier who was barking at her to come out again. But on her knee she had a book; it was open, and she was writing in it; and half of the book was full. She had got up early every morning that summer to write. And what she was writing was poetry – poetry in stanzas of four lines, irregular in length and accent, but rhymed alternately. She was happy. She was not unhappy now, or had not been a moment before; and in the feeling that possessed her while this picture stayed it would be impossible to divide pleasure from sadness, and both were pure and profound. She tried to remember some of the verses. They were about an oak tree. Grown-up people had told her they were not a mere senseless echo of some grown-up poet's emotion or words, as a precocious child's verses often are, but really seemed to shadow forth the child's impression of the life in the big Briareus tree with its strange silences and strange voices. For an instant she felt herself standing under the tree as a child, but she knew that she dreamed and in an instant, all was gone. The pictures ceased while she remembered simply the bliss which she had in those days not recognised. Then through that solemn haze of emotion many scenes reassembled again – a few people, rooms, gardens, fields, and streets, shadowy and precise, and strange too because all, animate and inanimate, were equally alive – like shapes moving or still, seen through softly drifting rain. Clearest of all was that child that had been herself, a bold, strong, original child – it could not be denied – passing through that large many-coloured world as if she had been the spirit of it all. Words were spoken, little words surviving like poems out of the ruins of a life; actions were performed. Books appeared, distinct passages, the very language often, and then also the pictures they had called up in that early time. Everything had given way to her in that year and the one that followed. The world was made for her, it was hers. How confidently she went about! what joy, what power! And she carried with her a secret – her personality, her self, what made her the equal of all men and things, even in a sense their superior, since she grasped them and did not feel herself grasped by them, not yet. She and her mother possessed the world. Her golden-haired mother she saw in one attitude always, seated, curved graciously forward, head slightly bowed, but eyes raised and fixed upon nothing of this world, unconscious that the child beside her was watching her through the hair which her fingers were tangling amorously; she also had her secret, a mighty mother she seemed, greatest of all the things that had life on earth, who yet had nothing to do but to love Alice who on her part had nothing to do but to give her occasions for love, for love and forgiveness. A greater painter than Titian had painted those people and those days. In their veins ran gold of June, and all about them was poured an equal holy light. It was to last and she was to live for ever. She had heard the word, and the meaning, of death, only to resolve that it was not in her destiny: she was even sure that no one with whom she was linked by any close bonds could pass away; upon everything was a seal of everlastingness.

Then a schoolroom, many books, grey books, books that rasped the hand and the soul, that were quite other than that fair world. Several of the years that followed were cut off, she knew not where or how, from those when she wrote poems: she wrote no more. She remembered other children, numbers of them, who were not as those of the earlier time, but as if they had come out of the grey books with which they were linked. She read the books and listened to men and women who explained them and asked her questions. She forgot continually, but was praised for what she retained, was given prizes and talked about in her own hearing as a clever child. She lost her secret; her mother had taken her own away and died. She still enjoyed many things but not as before; she had a sense of something postponed; the next day or perhaps the next the veil would be lifted that had fallen insiduously, a veil of huge, dim, unintelligible things, of mere greyness, having nothing to do with life but acquiesced in as in a disease, like which it brought its own opiate.

The veil was lifted, but underneath were not the colours of the regretted time; there was pain, weariness, misery, ending in illness from overwork. As she lay in bed she looked back as she was doing now. The weakness, silence, and solitude, the independence of the sick room, seemed about to restore the old time through the tears she wept quietly and long in thinking of the grey shameful years. Her window looked out upon the country and the spring, upon a shallow river rippling under alders, between meadows that rose gently up from it to the steep wooded hill which closed the view and shut out all of the sky, except a narrow indigo band against the dark trees and the firm snowy bases of the freshest white clouds she had ever seen. The alders had been lately cut to within two feet of the earth and their sharp gashed stems, moistened by rains, were orange; at their feet were primroses so numerous that she could see them as far as where the river wound out of sight. At the edge of the high woods, which were of pine and very dark, she could see shining almost white the breasts of the two missel-thrushes whose songs she heard, and of a wood-pigeon that had been there since dawn. Within the wood there was one bent silvery birch that seemed to her every time she looked at it to be a lost princess just about to run away from that immense dark host of pines. The sun burnished the white clouds, the grass now green for the first time in the year, the ripples at the curves of the river, and the breasts of the three birds. The missel-thrushes had repeated their wild sweet song over and over since she awoke. There was only one other sound and that was of the bees which she knew must be at the crocuses out of sight under her window. The air was moist, cold, pellucid and so pure that as the bees passed her window she thought she could smell their fragrant burdens. She was happy, or she was going to be very happy; she was expecting something which never appeared, and she thought she wanted someone to be near her. She called out but when someone came she knew there was no one she was willing to have; she sent for a doll she had not seen for three years and fell asleep with it before the missel-thrushes had ceased. That night she was ill again and near death.

Thinking now of the years of crawling convalescence, the arrested development, the slight curvature of the spine, the drooping eyelid (as if in that narrow room the prostrate child had been through all womanhood), thinking of the isolation, of the childless echoing house where she had rested a long bitter rest, of the little country town's one winding broad street – a flock of sheep pressed in between the high grey houses of melancholy stone, very silent – that passed at either end quite suddenly into the purest country of slow rivers and gradual hills, thinking of things almost of yesterday, Alice became fully awake and conscious of the organ music, and tried to put it away from her, but failed. Several times she dipped her fingers into the wet grass and bathed her eyes. Then she stood up straight, for a moment even on tiptoe, slowly let her head fall back, fully extended her arms with outstretched fingers, and drew in a long breath as if drawing in, with prayer and confidence, all the sweetness and strength of the air, and, afraid of the involuntary sigh of the expiration, began to walk rapidly down the hill.

She did not stop until she came to a cottage at the border of a green. The children had rooted out a bat and ball and some stumps, and with coats off were playing cricket for the first time in the year. She went round to the back of the cottage where a woman of equal massiness and agility was washing clothes in the open air, the hard white linen and the loose froth mimicking the heavy and the lighter clouds in the blue sky.

'Good morning, Mrs Appleyard,' said Alice.

'Good morning, miss,' replied the cloud-maker.

'What shall I do? play cricket with the boys or help you?'

'Won't you sit down, miss? 'Tis weariful weather. I feel myself as if I could sleep for a week. Still, 'tis beautiful weather, too.'

'Yes,' said Alice, lost for the moment in following Mrs Appleyard's magnificent energy, presently adding, 'How is the baby?'

'Wonderful well. Would you like to go up and see her? And Bessie would be glad to see you.'

In one of the two bedrooms in the attached cottage Mrs Appleyard's daughter lay in bed with her third child, new born. The coarse red-faced cowman's wife, now pale and languid, smiled faintly at Alice but let the smile expand into a broad chuckling grimace for the child to whom she turned immediately, excusing herself by saying, 'She's a beauty. We are calling her Catherine Elizabeth.'

'You're glad to have her, Bessie,' said Alice, smiling and taking up the child.

'I should think so, miss. You don't know. Don't you take any notice another time of what a woman says seven or eight months before her baby's born, when she doesn't want another. It's just nature. Still, there are mothers and mothers. Now my sister-in-law at Woodford has just had her fifth and, would you believe it? she's been asking the vicar if he knows anyone that wants a child. A pretty child, too – why, I'd like it myself, but, Lord, what would Bill say? – all that family's pretty, but this one is a white blackbird, as you might say.'

'Really,' said Alice, slowly, 'wants to give it away . . . or perhaps make a little money out of it. . . . Well, I don't wonder. Times are bad for workers. But does she really?'

'But you would wonder if you was a woman. I beg your pardon, I mean, you know what I mean. But in her it's unnatural. Only three months old, too.'

'Is it a boy or a girl?'

'A girl and the best of the bunch.'

'What is her name?'

'Rose Elizabeth, after me.'

'And it is quite healthy?'

'Yes, bless you, healthy, yes.'

'But wouldn't she want it back again, don't you think? Supposing she grew up in a good home now . . .'

'That's just what she wants. She'd make a little lady and no mistake. Some old couple, good people, gentry perhaps, would be glad of her if they only knew. They have their feelings, same as any of us.'

'And is her mother all right, except for this lack of affection?'

'Annie? Strong as a cart horse, a good-looking woman, too, in her way – she's Suffolk bred – but hard, or, well, the fact is she doesn't like Ted.'

'Your brother?'

'Yes.'

'Ah!'

Alice got up and looked out of the window at the lambs, which had been separated by hurdles from their mothers and turned into a great field of swedes, and were nibbling the tops of one and then another of the purple roots for a moment, lazily, and now and then sprawling down in the sun. She turned and asked:

'What does the vicar say, Bessie?'

'Oh, you're thinking of Annie's little Rose? He scolded her.'

'You don't think he has found anyone? I was thinking I knew, I might find, somebody who would be glad, who would consider it . . .'

'Yes, miss?'

'In fact you might mention it in case there is no one already considering it. Or I would write. My friend . . . the person I had in mind . . . I . . .'

Alice stayed a little longer, but hardly spoke, musing and pleased with the indolent pressure of the baby in her arms.

'That baby's all right, miss,' said Mrs Appleyard as Alice came out into the yard again, 'and Bessie's doing well. She'll be all the

better for the rest. Healthy women like her never gets any other rest, and having me close by she'll take a full fortnight.'
'And isn't she fond of the little one!'
'Fond! and why ever shouldn't she be, miss. There's naught the matter with our Bessie.'
'Yes, but she was telling me about her little niece, Rose Elizabeth.'
'Yes.'
'She says the parents are willing to let someone adopt the child and . . .'
'So they were. I didn't want to upset Bessie, miss, but little Rose fell off a chair . . .'
'Dead! not dead?'
'No, she hurt herself though. She will live, but they will have to keep her now.'
'Oh . . .' sighed Alice in the struggle between the suddenly swollen emotion and the shock and the wish to say something of the expected kind to Mrs Appleyard who went on:
'It's a judgment on them. Why do they want to go putting off the child on somebody they don't know?'
'Yes . . . No . . . It is very sad. A crippled child . . . Most people would not think of taking it, I suppose.'
'I should think not, miss.'
'But perhaps you would give me your son's address, Mrs Appleyard. I think my friend might still . . . thank you.'
She was going away when she picked up an egg-cup full of violets from the window-sill and said:
'Violets! how sweet! I haven't found any this late season. Where did you find them?'
'Mary found them. She always finds the first. You see she is so little that she looks the flowers in their faces almost. She is so fond of them and says she likes their "pale calm blue", funny little thing!'
'Good-bye, Mrs Appleyard.'
'Good morning, miss.'
Never before had the homeward hill seemed so long and steep as when Alice climbed back again, wearied, pulled to pieces, miserable over her new hope, her still newer despair, the scent of violets, and now . . . no! it was impossible . . . a crippled child, and a girl . . . Rose Elizabeth . . . its brain might have

been affected by the fall . . . And yet was it not already in a sense hers?

'I think, Alice,' said Colonel Lacking that evening, 'you had better have a sea voyage. We will take one together, I think. Yes. This English spring is too much for us when we are no longer young. You're looking a fright.'

'It's not the spring, father, it's myself.'

'Where shall it be?' he continued, looking at a map of this world.

Sunday Afternoon

'Fear of punishment,' read Mrs Wilkins, in a clear hard percussive tone like that of two flints being struck together: 'Fear of punishment has always been the great weapon of the teacher, and will always, of course, retain some place in the conditions of the schoolroom. The subject is so familiar that nothing more need be said of it. The same is true of *Love*, and the instinctive desire to please those whom we love. . . .'

Her voice burst through the ear into the brain as if with an actual physical presence, and the words themselves were apprehended dimly and fitfully like those of a man who guides us amid the whirr and hammer and throb of a factory. She held the book level with her eyes, which were for the most part fixed on the page as if it were a poor living thing whose life and death were in her power: when for a moment they were removed, it was without a change of expression, to some one of her audience of six who had seemed to betray inattention by a moving foot, a sigh, or a closing of the eyes in search of rest – vain search. Once she stopped and said to one child of the party, her granddaughter:

'Cathie, my pet, move your chair from behind your grandfather's, then you will not be so very near the fire and you will be able to see grandmother.'

Here she smiled by the mechanical act of pressing the middles of her thin lips together so as to elongate her mouth and protract the line of it upward into her grey lean cheeks. Then she continued to read with a frown at the book or at fate for having interrupted her, as in a short time happened once more. Her husband laid his huge kind hand silently upon his little grandchild's head, which it almost enclosed like the husk of a hazel nut, and there let it remain.

'Charles,' she said in the same tone, laying the book softly but firmly, and as it were cruelly, upon the black silk over her knees, 'do you really wish me to go on with this important book or not?'

'Why, yes, my dear,' he replied, instinctively smoothing the infant's hair to protect her and to encourage himself.

'Then may I ask you not to interrupt, and not to set Cathie a bad example by apparent inattention?'

'Please go on, my dear,' he said, removing the offending hand with a slight sigh of penitence and outward submission, and a twinkle of the unconquerable mind in the gay lifting of the brows over his large brown eyes that knew so well the arts of brotherhood, fatherhood, unclehood, and now for five years, of grandfatherhood.

'Then I will continue,' she said, with a rustling gesture of imperfect appeasement, 'or rather I will go back to the beginning of the chapter lest some of us should have forgotten it by this time.'

She read again: 'Fear of punishment has always been . . .' and complete silence was granted by everyone, and as far as possible by the hollow fire itself, which was now, in sympathy with the subdued audience and respect for its instructor, growing every minute more cold and black. The voice, absolutely monotonous, seemed to build an intricate structure of thin polished steel bars in the air, like a high bridge, but without obvious purpose. Most of the audience were, however, too well used to the sound to observe this effect.

Her husband was a country doctor now retired from his practice, a man with the profile of an aged Jupiter and straight white hair and beard, who had learned in forty years of marriage to live at the same time two lives, an outer one of many duties and ceremonies for the benefit of his wife, and an inner one into which she had neither the leisure nor the curiosity to inquire, even if it had once or twice occurred to her that there was such a thing. This afternoon he was chiefly occupied in recalling to his memory Shelley's poem of 'Rosalind and Helen'.

Three of the unmarried daughters were there. They were women of thirty-three, twenty-nine and twenty-five years of age, who spent nearly the whole of their year as governess, schoolmistress and private secretary, but came home regularly at about Christmas time to worship out of long habit the mother with whom they had no contact at any other time, except by sending half of their salaries for her to invest. They admired their mother's force of character, her power of management, her indifference to the flight of time, and her clear fatigueless voice. Nervous and intelligent they suffered from the voice and the tyranny, but they, like their father, were able to quench their suffering in memories and thoughts of the separate worlds unknown to her. One of them, indeed, gave a moment or two of real attention to the words that were said, because the book was her present to her mother and she hoped to be able to say a few intelligible words in any discussion that might follow. The faces of all three were lined and thin, their black hair was going grey, and all wore spectacles. They were older than their mother. Their bony painful hands were clasped tightly on their knees; their plain dresses were ruffled over their flat chests, their heads bent. Two at least would never marry now, for their mother's knowledge of men and her exacting standard, reinforced by that voice of steel, had made it impossible for them to give way to their desires, from which this discipline was never removed. When the reader turned her eyes upon them she was reassured by three pairs of spectacles glittering attention.

In the background was another visitor but an unconsidered one, a young artist of small independent means who was supposed to be in love with one of the daughters, no one knew which. He was tall, dark, slender, mild and obviously uncomfortable, but as he never lost this expression it was unobserved, and he also was well under Mrs Wilkins' control.

The little girl was the child of a daughter who had run away to marry. The maternal discipline was escaped only for a time. Letters, visits, and that omnipotent voice had never ceased to besiege the girl after her marriage. She had consented to leave her husband and to come to live with her parents again. There, one Christmas day, in a festive house, while the north-east wind from the sea drove the sand through fast shut windows on to the hair and the sheets, into the food, into the soul, she gave birth to a child who was at once taken over by its grandmother with the words:

'Poor Alice, you see, can know nothing of children any more than she can of men. I know. All will be well.'

Mrs Wilkins took up this new interest in her crowded life of visiting the poor, making jam and marmalade, and sewing for befriended unfortunate women, as eagerly as if it were the only one.

Alice could not look after her baby, but she could cook and give her mother's advice to the neighbouring cottagers' wives. She worked hard and was feverishly content with having Cathie close at hand; she acquiesced with a faint humorous smile in her mother's judgment, 'We shall hardly make a little lady of Cathie if she has much of her father's blood.' But she crumbled slowly under the strain of her too great self-despair and self-control. One day in the next winter, as she was shutting the oven door on a half shoulder of mutton, a strong thought came into her head. She told the maidservant that she was going to drown the old cat, which she put softly into a basket with some hay and left the house. It was the first day of a thaw: the grey world dripped and reeked and gurgled and the air made the warmest clothing seem to be lined with ice. An hour later the villagers were hurrying past the house, saying that a woman had drowned herself in the river.

'What a day for her to choose, to be sure!' remarked Mrs Wilkins. 'Poor thing! I wonder who it can be. The poverty in the village is dreadful at this time of year, and there is no religion worthy of the name except in my little band. A love affair, perhaps. Why didn't she come to me? That is the pity of life – that we can't give others the full advantage of our experience. Each one wants to start afresh. The young must needs be running off to get experience for themselves, when if they only asked. . . . Look at Alice, for example. She knew nothing about men: how should she? But if she had come to me. . . .'

Then she pursed her lips with a short smile, adding thereto, as a gesture expressing modest approval of her own kindly thought, a nod of singular bird-like prettiness – for her figure and head were of exquisite regularity and proportion, well-carried and dressed with unvarying grace.

It was Alice that lay in the river, dead, with a satisfied expression. The cat came running home miserable, tiptoe on wetted paws.

Mrs Wilkins' grief at the suicide was tempered and at last quenched in a grave wondering why it should have happened, and she therefore acquiesced in the verdict of 'during temporary insanity'. 'I cannot believe it,' she said at the first news, 'she dared not.' And 'I could hardly believe my eyes,' she continued to say when describing the scene, which she would do in the same manner as when she recited. 'The Assyrian came down like a wolf on the fold,' or, 'Little lamb, who made thee?'

'Now Cathie is ours to make a great success of,' said Mrs Wilkins. 'That father of hers was at any rate a strong man and she inherits his physique. As for her character, I see she has the very ways of my own sister, little Bess who died young. She would have been the best of us all, and she was as clever as she was good. She overworked herself, Charles! and died out of her mind, poor thing; and she had a love affair, too; a young man pestered her with his objectionable affections and she was too weak to reject them altogether as we could have wished, and it was too much for her. But Cathie is strong and she will be with me.'

For a few years, nevertheless, Cathie was snatched away to live in London with her father in a golden age of health and wilfulness, four years that would be a possession for ever, the richest jewel in a happy life, a crown lying at the bottom of the well of an unhappy one. But her father died and, after being passed from relative to relative, she had now arrived at her grandmother's by the sea.

At first Cathie feared the sea because there were no roads on it, and the moors round the house also, because there were no pavements on which she could get to avoid the cows. Things were too large. The earth was as large as the sky. But, on the other hand, there were black cattle and windmills on the glittering wide marsh below the house, and there was always a flock of starlings wheeling over the heather close to the door, or perched in a row on the single telegraph wire humming over the line of posts that seemed to come out of the sky – with messages from her father, perhaps, mused the child. Also there was a most ancient man who leaned against a sunny bank, as still as a tree but with a cheerful face that was chiefly eyes and whiskers like some very nice dog, clothes that were more like an animal's coat than any she had ever seen before, and a growl of a voice which somehow she knew to be kind when he said, 'Good morning, little miss, a pretty morning, little miss!' She liked walking in the little oak wood on the cliffs at the edge of the sea, where the dead leaves raced down the steep path as the rats ran after the pied piper of Hamelin, and then suddenly whirled up like butterflies and almost smothered her. On the beach there were many pebbles, and she thought that if she did a little work daily she would be able to finish a house by the time when she would wear spectacles as her aunts did, and there she could invite 'Gyp' the dog and 'Tansy' the cow and kill anybody else who tried to get in – no! not quite kill them because if they were dead they would be like her father and nobody deserved to be like that. But next day there was not a trace of her pebbles nor any footmarks of the thief, so perhaps it was her father and he was making the house in some better place.

The day after was Sunday and it was sufficiently near Christmas for sweets and nuts to be eaten in the sitting-room after dinner. She curled up in a warm chair and stared at the fire and ate continuously while the others talked and laughed more than usual, and her grandfather pitched a special sweet now and then into her lap and evidently did not want her to say, 'Thank you, dear grandpapa' before she put it into her mouth. One of her aunts played on the piano and Cathie still stared at the fire, warm and drowsy and sniffing the fruit, the wood fire, the scents of the women, and listening to the wind. She saw beautiful rockets rising straight up and spreading out like a palm tree among the stars, just as on the night before her father died. By and by the trees ceased to grow and an enormous bird stood on the earth and touched the sky: it had eyes all along its immense beak and all down its long legs, so that it could see everything as her grandmother had told her God could; so for fear lest the bird should take her last sweet she bolted it and began to cough, whereupon her grandmother said in a voice that came shooting through the music:

'Cathie, my pet, you are disturbing your aunt and spoiling our pleasure. You must not always be thinking of yourself.'

'I was thinking of God, grandmamma,' she said, but the music drowned her words. The great bird was gone, and she wished she had not swallowed the sweet because she had meant to give it to 'Tansy'. She sobbed a little and slept.

She was awakened by her grandmother telling her to sit in another chair and keep quiet while she read aloud. Again she saw the palm trees of fire, and when the golden fruit showered down there was a helter skelter of dead leaves to save themselves from being burnt, and they ran into a house made of pebbles such as she had begun to build on the beach. Now and then she heard the voice of her grandmother who was reading from a book about angels and war, which appeared to be a wicked book, but she understood little except certain familiar words – the word 'victor', for example, reminded her of a little boy of that name and she was all ear for what followed, but in vain.

These thoughts were interrupted by her grandfather saying quietly for the second time that he could not hear, and her grandmother laying down the book and saying: 'Charles, I am reading for your pleasure, and I do think it is inconsiderate of you to interrupt . . . I think I will read a little from my own book now, Jenny's present.'

Mrs Wilkins took up the other book and read, 'Fear of punishment has always been the chief weapon of the teacher . . .' twice over, telling Cathie to sit in another chair farther from the fire.

For some time Cathie thought about nothing, and then again tried to puzzle out who had disturbed her pebbles and fancied the great bird had picked them up in his great beak, and she hoped he would swallow them and choke and be reprimanded by her grandmother. In her new seat she could see the young man, and wished she could show him her doll which was upstairs.

When the reading was over the young man rose up and looked kindly at her, and said he would go to his room and read.

Cathie looked out of the window at the moor which was now almost dark, and said to everyone:

'Why do those trees look like *that*?'

They smiled but made no reply, Jenny alone remarking, 'How sweet children are.' Mrs Wilkins was saying that they would now sing some hymns, each one choosing a favourite, when Cathie got up to follow the young man and, seeing the door shut loudly behind him, burst into tears at the thought of him and her doll both out of reach in the winter darkness. So wide opened her eyes and so far fell her mouth, so loud was her crying, that her grandmother was angry as she sat down at the piano and began to turn over the pages of the hymn book. The sound of the crying brought back the young man, and he offered to take her to his room.

'That is very kind of Mr Cardew,' said Mrs Wilkins. 'Do you hear, Cathie? But I think, Harry, she ought not to go. It is so bad for her to have her own way.'

'Then you shall sit on my knee, Cathie,' said Mr Cardew, in a vaguely protective gentle voice, not without hostility to the ruling power. He sat down and took her on his knee and encircled her as much as possible with his shoulders and both arms. She ceased to cry but not to sob and to twist the world into a tragic agony with the falling corners of her mouth, her huge eyes and lifted eyebrows of surprise.

The first hymn began:

> Shepherd Divine, our wants relieve
>   In this our evil day:
> To all Thy tempted followers give
>   The power to watch and pray.
> Long as our fiery trials last,
>   Long as the cross we bear,
> O let our souls on Thee be cast
>   In never-ceasing prayer. . . .

It was the choice of one of her aunts. Cathie sobbed all through it: her sweet breath rose up to her protector and her convulsive movements shook the hymn book which he absent-mindedly watched, and shook her little head and raven curls so that she could see and think of nothing but her grandmother's icy spectacles and moving lips. At the end of each verse the aunts and grandfather glanced at her furtively. When five hymns had been sung, Cathie still sobbed and shook, and Mrs Wilkins offered to let the child choose the next instead of her.

'Now, Cathie, my pet,' she said, using the tone which she had always supposed to be soothing and endearing, 'which is your favourite? "Christ who once amongst us as a child did dwell"?'

Cathie sobbed and made no reply. She was wondering why her grandmother's spectacles looked grim as the trees outside, 'like *that*.' Mrs Wilkins continued:

'Shall it be "All things bright and beautiful," or, "Do no sinful action, speak no angry word"? . . . What was father's favourite?'

Cathie did not hear, for the spectacles were still icy and grim.

'Then I will choose for you, dear,' concluded Mrs Wilkins, removing the notes of soothing and endearment from her voice; and so they sang:

> Our God of love who reigns above
>   Comes down to us below;
> 'Tis sweet to tell He loves so well,
>   And 'tis enough to know. . . .

At the end Mrs Wilkins said judicially:

'I think Cathie ought to be very thankful to us all for singing to her when she was a disobedient child. But she had better go early to bed now. Perhaps she is very tired. . . . Kiss everyone "Good-night", Cathie. . . . Good-night, child.'

One of her aunts led her away.

'She has her mother's temper,' said Mrs Wilkins. 'Her mother was just like that. I am afraid we shall have some trouble in bringing her up as we should like, but I do not despair, Charles.'

'No, my dear,' said Mr Wilkins, not convinced that by graduating grandmother a woman became wise.

'No, she makes me feel young again,' continued his musing hopeful spouse, 'and I will bring her up as if she were one of my own.'

Cathie sobbed upstairs, and that evening it was as if the sea, and the wind on the moor and in the keyholes, were sobbing with her, until at last she slept. The wind ceased and all the house was still. About midnight she woke again to see through her window the small bright moon flying up through snowy clouds over the sea. It seemed to her that it was the very same moon she used to see at her father's house, and she smiled and slept happily.

Milking

The end of April was sappy, careless, and profuse. One day it was all eagerness and energy and gave no rest to the wind and the sun, on the earth or in the waters or in the clouds of the sky, and the songs of the birds were a mad medley. Another day it was indolent: a soft grey sky without form covered all; there was no wind; the birds were still; the lusty, buxom spring, a pretty and merry slut, with her sleeves and skirts tucked up and her hair down over her eyes and shoulders, had fallen asleep in the midst of her toil and nothing could waken her but a thunderstorm in the night. The next day she was simply at play with showers and sunlight, sunlight and showers, at play with sky and earth as if they were but coloured silks and now she fluttered the white and blue and green together and then, wearying of that, held up the grey and the grey-white and the green, and lastly mingled all together inextricably. For the most part she preferred not to let either go quite out of sight; when the heavy rain fell on the rustling wood it was out of a sky serene, lustrous, and mild; and when the light was steady and the rain tripping away from it upon myriad feet down among the leaves to the earth, still the shadows of the rain clouds stole over the hills like smoke. There was a gamesome spirit abroad. It was seen in the amorous conflict of rain and sun, and heard in the cry of the titmouse along the hedge: 'Fitchy! fitchy!'

Rain or not, always far away in the south there was a cluster of white peaks apparently belonging to a land that knew neither our sun nor our rain. Rain or sunshine or both made little difference to the shed at the cross roads. It was shadowy and old under a roof that was patched and hollowed like the sail of a ship. The door was open, but on either side the piles of dung were high and long and allowed the sun to enter the shed only for half an hour each day. And now in that half-hour the farmer Weekes was going to milk the last of his seven cows. Until now he had known of the afternoon only that the wind whined in the roof and that the rain dripped through on to his back at intervals. When the sun at last stepped in between the banks of dung he could see that it was a forward spring. For his eye travelled up between the green walls of the road to the hills four miles away, and there the beech trees were almost in perfect leaf and in their dense ranks resembled a flock of sheep with golden fleeces descending the slope. Yet it wanted a week before May-day. The grass was good, and already the cows were clean and bright after their winter in the yard; and, having looked at his hands alongside the white and strawberry hide of the cow, he got up and wiped them on a wisp of grass beside the door. He stood there a moment – a tall, crooked man, with ever-sparkling eyes in a nubbly and bony head, worn down by sun and toil and calamity to nothing but a stone, hollowed and grey, to which his short black hair clung like moss; in his starved fields you might have found a weathered flint of the same shape, and have said that it was much like a man's head. He stretched himself, and then turned and called the cow by her name in a voice so deep and powerful that it was as if the whole shed and not a man's chest had uttered it.

He sat down again to milk and to think, with his face turned to the sun. He was thinking of the farmhouse under those woods on the hill, where he used to go courting twenty years ago, and of the girl, the only daughter of that house, who was now his wife. He had driven over there one day in his father's cart to see about some pigs. The old man had given him supper, honey and bread and butter, cold apple dumplings with cheese, and cowslip wine. It was a wonderful quiet house, very dark under tall beeches, with a quality in the dark still air as if it were under water, but very clean and bright with china and brass and the white tablecloth and the old man's white beard and glittering blue eyes. He knew that the old man was failing to make both ends meet, but there was no sign of it, and he spoke with a cheerful gravity, and there was a look about house and man as if they were apart from the world, and not subject to such accidents as failure of crops, cattle disease, and the like. They had done their business, and at the end of a long silence he was thinking of rising to go, when Emily, the daughter, came in without noticing him, kissed her father, and said, 'Father, there is a white bird in the old apple tree of the rick-yard singing like a blackbird. Yet 'tis as white as milk.'

'Well, we will all come and see,' said the old man, and then she saw that a stranger was there, and with a blush she retreated and opened the door. As she was shutting it she turned round out of curiosity, thus revealing her own face to the stranger, but seeing nothing of his which was in shadow. In a minute or two they went out into the rickyard where the cart was waiting. Emily was patting the horse's neck, but with her face towards the old apple-tree where a white blackbird was singing from the topmost branch. 'You will not let them shoot it, father, will you?' she said. The white bird and its song, the girl's fair hair, and rosy face very serious, the unbent old man soon to die, the sombre smouldering old tiles and brick wall of the house, and the high black woods behind, were remembered now. Soon afterwards he had returned to the house, and again and again, avowedly to see Emily. In the late summer they used to walk out after the haymaking was all over, while the nightjar sang and the woods were dark and discreet and the sky above them as pale green as a new-mown field. They went in amongst the untrodden bracken together. He could recall the smell of the crushed fronds where they sat, the light of the near planet between the fox-gloves gushing from the violet sky, and the kisses that were as sweet as the honeysuckle overhanging them, and, unlike that, could be tasted again and again without cloying.

And now the cold whine of the wind in the roof and the drop of the rain, and Emily was lying at home, sick, with a dead new-born child in the next room, and a child that he was glad was dead, yes! that even she would not be crying after if she knew what a monstrous mistaken thing had come into the world with their help. Weekes looked at that old farmhouse and the rickyard, the crushed bracken bower, as if to search among these things engraved by joy upon his brain for the devilish magic that had brought about this wretchedness. He looked at her remembered face, scanning it for something to explain this thing, looked closely and fiercely at the face that was turned back towards him in her father's doorway so that he loved her from that day. What? Why? But neither in the young girl nor in the worn woman could he see what he sought. He thought of their labours, of the six children she had borne and reared, of her rough hands and wrenched voice, of the smearing out of all her prettiness except her hair. He turned it over and over, ruminating, undisturbed by the spurting of the milk into the pail, the trickle of the shower, or the sight of the hills and the clouds over the hills. Yet he did not take his eyes off these hills, nor change the look given to them by his pain and questioning – questioning he knew not what now – the whole order of things, perhaps, from which the terror had sprung unexpected. Having naught for his brain to grip and hold, but only the dead ghastly child lying still, and repeating the question, and round about it the moving world of men and Nature, enormous and endless and careless, each effort was weaker than the last and sorrow brought its narcotic stupidity. It was some time after he had drawn her last milk that the cow licked his face impatiently. He kicked away the stool and began singing a verse of a ribald song which he did not know he had remembered –

> Poor Sally's face is plain
> But Sally's heart is kind –

And it was so singing that, without wishing it, he returned the question to the teeming womb and grave of the earth, to be swallowed up in the vast profusion of life and death, while the merry maid waved to and fro the coloured silks of the sunshine and of the rain, and the titmouse crept through the hedge, crying, waggishly, 'Fitchy! fitchy!'

THE FLOWER-GATHERER

'Herself a fairer flower.' – MILTON

SO STRONG was the young beauty of the year, it might have seemed at its height were it not that each day it grew stronger. The new day excelled the one that was past, only to be outshone by the next. Day after day the sun poured out a great light and heat and joy over the earth and the delicately clouded sky. The south wind flowed in a river straight from the sun itself, and divided the fresh leaves with never-ceasing noise of amorous and joyful motion. So mighty was the sun that the miles of pale new foliage shimmered mistily like snow, yet each leaf was cool and moist with youth, and the voices of the birds creeping and fluttering among the branches were as the souls of that coolness and moistness and youth. If one moment the myriad forms of life and happiness intoxicated the delighted senses, at another a glimpse of the broad mild land stretched out below, and of the sun ruling it in the blue above, gave also a calm and a celestial dignity and simplicity to the whole. One after another the pools, the rivers and rivulets, the windows or glass roofs of the vale, caught the sun and sparkled as if Vega and Gemma and Arcturus and Sirius and Aldebaran and Algol had fallen among the meadows and woods.

On some days the sense of oneness, of wide power and splendour uniting earth and sky, of infinite simplicity, triumphed. On others the spirit was content to bathe and half lose itself in numbers, exuberance, complexity, in the odours and colours and forms, one by one, in the rich rising flood of the grass, in the hurrying to and fro of preparation that was nevertheless not over much troubled about the end.

The children seemed to be trying to gather all the flowers. It was their way of striving to grasp the infinite. They were scattered over the hillside, where the pale sward was made an airy or liquid substance by the innumerable cowslips nodding upon its surface, as upon a lake, that held their small shadows each quite clear. All day they gathered flowers, and threw them away, and gathered more, and still there were no less. The earth continued to murmur with blissful ease, as if, like the wandering humble bee, it were drowsed with the warmth and the abundance.

One child separated herself from the rest, moving down instead of across or up the hill. Often she went on her knees among the flowers, with bent eyes that saw only the hundreds close at hand. But from time to time she raised her head, her delicately browned and yet more rosy face, her gleamy hair, that was as pale as barley on her temples but elsewhere golden brown as wheat, her round and calm yet lively eyes, her restless happy lips – and looked steadily for a moment at the whole of earth and sky, and grew solemn, only to return to the other pleasure of the hundred cowslips just at her feet, the crystal and emerald wings among them, the pearly snails, the daisies and the chips of chalk like daisies. Tighter grew her hand round the swelling bunch. She slipped; the flowers fell and not all were picked up again; and so there was yet room for bluebells when she reached the wood below. In the moister fields still lower there were kingcups of gold and cuckoo flowers pink and white, looking as if they had fluttered down from the sky; and for these also a place had to be found. The stitchworts of a hedge side lured and piloted her to the hollow, hardly larger than a great hall, where a brook ran straight, for once in its life.

By the slow stream forget-me-nots made a continuous haze on either bank. She was now quite alone, under the old cherry tree of the forsaken garden at the water's edge. Six or eight huge crooked branches rising out of the rocky trunk bore up a dome that was all flowers. They were in rounded clusters as of bubbling snow, and close as honeycomb. The lovely freckled white smelt bitter and sweet at once. The flowers hummed with bees, and between the clusters were streaks and wedges of the blue. The child looked up suddenly at this glorious roof, and her smile of surprise passed into what would have been indifference, because the blossoms were inaccessible, if she had not caught sight of the forget-me-nots when the flight of a cuckoo that had been calling out of the cherry-tree carried her eyes away to where he skimmed the water. He did not fly far, nor cease to call while he was flying, or when he was seated on one of the alders by the brook. She looked at him as she was plucking the forget-me-nots. This narrow hollow was his room, she thought. Yet it was full of other songs. There were blackbirds hidden in the hazels, or clearly defined against the may flower or the bronzed flowering oaks. Thrushes talked and called out to her a hundred times: 'Did she do it? Did she do it? Did she? Did she? She did, she did!' and she laughed. A swallow flew over his image in the water as if about to dive in after it, and then rose up and curved away. Smaller unfamiliar birds sang rillets and minute cascades of hurrying song. The gold-crest repeated a tune like the unwinding of a tiny sweetly-creaking winch, like the well-winch at home. But the lazy cuckoo was lord of all.

Now she had filled both hands, and each time she grasped a new stalk some of the old fell out. So presently she laid them down in the grass to rearrange them. But she now noticed the tall sedges of the brook and wanted some. She looked round to see if anyone could see her doing this forbidden thing, and then went to the edge and stretched out her hand: they were too far. The water was gliding under her, flashing like brandished steel, and yet as clear as air over the green stars of its bed. Everything had always been kind to her, and this water was one of the kindest, so playful and bright, so pure that sometimes they came far to fetch some of it in a pail for the house. She leaned out, and even moved one foot as if to step towards the green sedge. She lost her footing and fell, not quite reaching the blades as she splashed. She was scolded for getting wet, but never much, and she used to laugh as they were dressing her in fresh clothes; and to-day it was so warm. . . . It was an adventure. But her hair was all wet; she did not like that: and the water, though so pure, was not pleasant in mouth, nostrils, eyes, and ears, nor could she get rid of it. Her hands touched the green stars; she could see them; but the sky was gone. She was surprised, indignant, anxious to be out. Why this cruelty? It was not a game to go on like this. She was angry . . . terrified . . . numbed. She could see nothing but water, she heard, smelt, breathed, tasted, touched water everywhere. Who could have done it? Something is cruel! . . . Why? . . . She could not bear it. No! No! Where were her flowers? Where was her mother?

She rose up a little, and saw the sun, and the cuckoo on the branch through the waves, and heard the man calling to his horses in the next field. Then solitude: all pleasure gone, love, light, warmth, movement was nothing, was over there, was past, or never had been, would never be again. It was better now. Sleep, sleep. But in the sleep, songs, visions of the house, forms and faces moving to and fro, and herself going in and out amongst them, far away, long ago, over there, in that other place. She was hurrying faster and faster, running too fast for her legs, carried away off them into the air, but swaying and rising easily and more easily now. She sighed as she seemed to float higher and lighter into soft darkness, into utter darkness, into nothing at all, where there was never anything or will be anything. The mud settled down. The stream flowed clear and sweet. The sun had not so much to do but that he could wilt the flowers lying on the bank. Life went on exuberant, joyous, august, looking neither to the right nor to the left. The cuckoo called. The birds' songs became so drowsy that they were not missed when they ceased, and only its own echo replied to the cuckoo. The child's white forehead was just above the water, and a fly perched on it and preened his diamond wings. A quarter of a mile away the dinner bell at home was swung merrily again and again by a strong arm that enjoyed the task.

Home

A LITTLE square sitting room, not very high, and hardly wider than it was high, yellow-lit by a brass lamp in the centre, and shutting out the visible world by three walls of a pleasant dull gold and indistinguishable pattern, and by three narrow curtains of a ruddiness that was dreamily heavy and sombre. On the walls, five pictures at the same height above the tops of the dark chairs, the mantelpiece and the sideboard; and on one, three shelves of books. A very still, silent room; and in it, motionless as in amber, a man standing before the books, and a woman with raised eyebrows and stiff but unquiet hands, dovetailed together, staring into the black-crusted fire. The man, chin on one hand, elbow on the other, tall and upright and dark like a pinnacle of black rock, looking sternly out of kind eyes at the books as at children. The woman, trying to drowse herself through her eyes by the fire and through every pore of her body by the silentness, yet aware all the time of the husband between her and the windows, as though his shadow blackened her instead of half the books. These two, separate and careful not to look at one another. Had they been utterly alone they would hardly have looked thus. They were not alone. In the stillness and silence, despite the walls and curtains, there was another presence, and a greater than they. It was London, a presence as mighty as winter, though as invisible. Its face was pressed up against the window; its spirit was within. And there was yet another, almost invisible, and as frail as the other was mighty – the spirit of the one who saw the room and felt the enchantment of London upon it. Neither the man nor the woman knew what was this second spirit in their room, yet the room was its home. It was the spirit of a young soldier dying in a far land. He was calm and easy now, without pain and without motion. Only his dark eyes told that he lived. As still was he, with bright fixed eyes, as a bird sitting on its nest. One had just left him who had spoken a few words intended to comfort him; but all the words had faded as soon as spoken, just as wavelets on a burning sand which they do not even stain, all except 'for your country'. He had heard these before without considering them, though he would have struck the man who mocked at them. This time they remained because they instantly recalled the first time he had heard them used, eighteen years before. His father had said to him one morning, 'Johnny, I am going to take you to see your country, to-morrow.' His pale mother had smiled her patient, weary smile – with some gentle ridicule added – at these words. Then she looked admiringly at her husband, the big, gaunt wry-faced man, whose eyes laughed so under his black brows. She had no country. She was born in the great city where they lived, where Johnny was born, and she had never left it. Nearly everything outside her home inspired her with wonder, awe, or fear, and she held her husband in awe because he had a country of which he frequently talked, where they spoke a different language, had queer names, different food, different ways and, as she dimly conjectured, a kind of common life as of one big family. Her husband had told her often that he had only to take a train to his country and get out at any station over the border, and somebody, most likely a cousin, would step up as if he had been waiting, and say, with his face all cut up by a smile, 'And how are you, David John, this long time?' But somehow he never went until this April. He had had to be content with talking, with taking the boy on his lap and singing the songs of his country, grand wailing songs that would often make him happy for the rest of the evening, merry, quick songs that made him tap the ground with his toes and yet brought tears into his eyes, so that he set the child down and went out into the street and came home, bitterly, hours afterwards to the dark house and the meek waiting wife.

But now he was really going to his country. 'To-morrow,' he said, 'we will take the train at midnight, and before noon we will be finding a curlew's nest on the moor just by where the old battle was.'

'What battle, father?' said the boy.

'Why, one of the old battles when we beat the English, I suppose,' said he.

'But what was the name of it, and when was it fought?'

'Ah, I cannot tell you that now: it is not in the history books. But the river there is called the River with the Red Voice, and there is a battle mound. The air is so clean there that a collar lasts you a fortnight.'

'Dear me,' said his mother, waking with a start from her musing.

Then the boy fell a-dreaming about his father picking up mottled eggs among dead men's bones by a river that ran red with blood.

Those bright eyes in the hospital tent saw now the railway station like a huge palace, sprinkled with lights and paved with multitudes of men and women, and good silent trains stretched out among them which the people had caught by a hundred handles and were mounting, to persuade them to carry them far off into the black night beyond, the unmapped black night with its timorous lines of small lights. He and his father entered the multitude and crept in and out alongside the train; and it was very wonderful, but many of the groups who talked were talking in the tongue in which his father used to sing, and he looked up at their pallid faces and black hair and agitated smiles and boldly moving lips, and was inclined to be afraid, but remembering that they were his father's people he was not afraid, but filled with wonder and admiration. Even some very little children, smaller than himself, were chattering in that same tongue quite easily; it seemed to Johnny that they were very clever little children. How kind everybody looked now! He had never seen so many people smiling and talking friendly before.

'Where is our country now?' said Johnny, and as soon as he had sat down with his face towards the land of his desire, the train was gliding out past a hedge of white faces and white lifted hands into the darkness.

The carriage was full, and the boy liked pressing up against his countrymen on both sides and touching their boots with his toes, and watching the thoughts on their faces and the books and papers they were reading, and how they would sometimes let their books and their papers fall on their laps, and look out at the wild-starred night seriously as if, perhaps, 'it had come . . . their country.' In a corner opposite sat a young woman, and next her a young man. He was reading. She was doing nothing but thinking, with her eyes turned towards Johnny. Soon the man closed his eyes; his head sank upon the woman's shoulder, but she did not move, only took away the book lest it should fall, and she offered Johnny a sweet, but he was too busy looking at her, and would not take it. The young woman's brown eyes fixed on him softly, and, his father's arm round him, he began to dream; and he awoke, surprised that he had been asleep, at a cold glittering station with a few faces staring in from the platform, looking for seats. 'Is this –?' He was going to ask his father if they had arrived, but he saw the name of a well-known town on the seats and lamps and again closed his eyes; the others also had looked and immediately closed their eyes. Then nothing – tiny lamps in the darkness – nothing again – then over a hill a large moon began to light a watery sky, black cloud and blacker earth, and looked afraid of the huge world over which she reigned. Another stop, a well-known name on the lamps, and then sleep to the sound of the train expressing steadiness, determination, and content in its rhythm and hope in its speed. If he opened his sleepy lids he saw the young woman's soft eyes, and the earth now grey and not black, and the moon high, without a cloud around or below, with groups of houses lost – as it seemed – in the night and cowering under the trees, here and there a light burning where someone, perhaps, was enviously watching the train on its march of discovery and conquest; or, still later, a pale sky lit from below and behind, as well as from the now invisible moon above, a river gleaming, a horse knee-deep in white mist looking up at the train, a church upon a hill that seemed awake but alone, small contemptible stations where they did not stop.

The fixed bright eyes in the bed saw these stations again in their dreariness, and saddened with the dream that he now was upon such a station, and the lighted train was rushing by and forgetting him, with its proud freight of living men looking ahead towards their country.

Nodding awake again, he saw the girl eating an orange, a wide water like a sea and the pale moon shrivelled beyond it, a farm and its cattle streaming out under a hill covered with crooked oaks, and the cattle were bowed under the weight of their long horns. 'It is near,' whispered his father: he slept.

When he awoke he was upon his father's knee, and both with cheeks together were looking, over frosty meadows and blown trees, at sand hills and sea beyond, and on the other side at hills crimsoned with bracken, their summits invisible, so steep were they. 'This is it,' said the father. 'Yes,' whispered the son, and both looked through and beyond the mountains and the sea to their country, the country of their souls, so that the child's first thought – that this was not what he had expected – never appeared again, until now in the tent. When a gap in the near hill showed them greater giants beyond that appeared to have descended out of the sky, and only half descended as yet, for their crests were in the clouds, the two were not more moved; they could see, far beyond these distances, greater hills, a land even more free.

They stopped, and there were wizard faces waiting, and the strange tongue that was the boy's own was spoken, and they seemed to welcome him. He began to step down from his father's knee to get out – but no, not yet.

They stopped again where there was only a black-bearded, tall man and a sheep-dog waiting. They could hear the thrushes sing, under the clear blue and the lightless moon, from out of dark thickets in a hollow rushy land, backed by the sea and the orange sails of vessels that caught the dawn. 'Over there,' said his father, pointing beyond the ships, 'is the land we have come from.' It was as faint and grey and incredible in the distance as his own land was clear and true; and he sighed with happiness and security, and also with anticipation of the further deeps that were to be revealed, the battlefield, the curlew's eggs, the castles, the harps, the harpers harping all the songs of his father. He had got so used to the faces of the men, which were like his father's, that when his father asked him whether they were not different from the English, he said 'No,' and was scolded for it.

The sun and the bright world dazzled his eyes. He slept. Then, a black barren land, a host of tall black chimneys between hills and sea, fountains of black smoke, sheaves of scarlet flame, red-hot caves. . . . Young men crowded into the carriage and burst out into a song. It was in the language that Johnny spoke, but the beauty of their voices in harmony made it different from anything he had heard before that day.

A marsh and a thousand sheep, gaunt hills on one side, sea on the other, and the young men singing a war march in their own tongue at his father's request. It made him afraid at first. Then he fancied that the battlefield was not far off, and they were going to it, and the song was sung to hearten a host of which he was one. He felt grim, but glad and bold as he looked at the dark young men and thought of 'his country'.

'My country,' muttered the dreamer lying still, and blinked his eyes as the tent flapped and he saw outside the sun of another country blazing and terrible as a lion above the tawny hills. The country that he had been fighting for was not this solitude of the marsh, the mountains beyond, the farms nestling in the beards of the mountains, the brooks and the great water, the land of his father and of his father's fathers, of those who sang the same songs, the young men and the old, and the women who had looked kindly on him. Where were those young men scattered? Where had their war march on that April morning led them?

A grim, black-bearded face was bending over him, with smiles deeply entrenched all over it. He was lifted straight into a cart behind a chestnut pony with his father and the man.

The sun was hot. They climbed up high among the hedgeless and pathless mountain, always up. The larks sang. The mountain lambs skipped before the cart.

They alighted by a solitary cottage under the road, whence a maid brought ale for the men and milk for the boy. They sat down among gorse bushes and ate apple tart and cheese, wafers of oat and currant cakes. The men talked. Johnny wandered up from the road with a girl of the cottage. And there with the rough strange mountain boys they set fire to the gorse and dead bracken. The flames leapt up like the genii out of the imprisoning jar in the Arabian tales, and he drew back. The earth was crowded with little flickering plants of fire spreading this way and that. Huge whirls and rounds of the yellow-white smoke soared up against the milky sky. The smell of the smoke heated by fire and sun was delicious. When the earth was black they moved on, while some sent the grey boulders galloping downward till they bounded over the road with a hero leap, and struck sparks out of other boulders or plunged into the gorse. The boys roared, the girls shrieked. All disappeared. But all day they could see the smoke of one conflagration pouring upwards before the wind in a great river, lost awhile in the hollows, seen again continually surging towards the high crests mile after mile, like a gigantic engine smoking wildly over the wilds.

Outside one cottage there stood a little old man, naked to the waist, washing himself and talking to three foxes chained up to a shed. The foxes seemed to understand his tongue and he theirs, and neither heeded the cart as it drove on. And now, careless of waterfalls thundering among low woods beneath the road, of flames and smoke clouds hunting upwards over the moor, and of mountains such as he had dreamed lying across their course a day ahead, Johnny fell asleep, content, not even rousing himself to make sure whether that was the cuckoo he heard upon the hillside.

The dream of the fixed open eyes wreathed and wavered. Was it the same day – it was morning and about noon – when he stood by the door of a long white inn fronting the sun? The wide courtyard, bounded on one side by the road and on the other by a green hedge, was dotted with fowls pecking idly or lying down. In the midst rose a brown oak, very thick and stiff and well stricken in years, and at its side a very tall gentleman with a fishing-rod was mounting a trap; and the boy watching him and thinking of his wealth and happiness was happier than he. On the hot white pavement by the door all the dogs were lazy in the sun. Each one, except the big, smooth pointer, had a bone, and each snarled as the pointer strolled past. There was a greyhound, a spaniel, a sheep-dog with one eye almost white, a mongrel, resembling both the spaniel and the pointer, and a fox-hound. From time to time the spaniel's puppies – pure spaniels – broke in among the fowls, and the mother raised her head and left the bone under her paws until the pointer re-appeared. It seemed to Johnny that the sun was always full upon that white inn, that the dogs were always lying down there in the sun, and that it had been so and would be so for all time. He longed to have an inn with a white wall facing the sun, and many dogs to take the sun upon the pavement in front. The fisherman drove away.

The father and son walked in a solitary wood upon the side of a steep hill, and at the foot of it was a green vale that wound with the windings of a broad stream running fast, and at the top of the hill, where it was a precipice, hung a castle with trees growing in its crevices, and its windows looked out through ivy thicker than its vast walls down at several miles of the green vale on either hand, at the sun-bathed gloom of the oakwoods of the opposite slope, at the other castles, bleached crags which could be recognised as the work of men only because they were even bolder and more gaunt than the natural crags round about. Sometimes it rained, sometimes the sun shone, and the father and son were glad of both as they gathered blue violets and white sorrel in the dripping and glistening woods. Under the castle wall they sat down, and the father brought out a book and read: 'King Arthur was at Caerlleon upon Usk . . .' and Johnny began to think of bowmen shooting through the ivy about the windows, of king and queen walking in the grassy courts within the walls, whose roof was the sky. His father told him that the book was written by his countrymen about the heroes of his country, and the child made over to those heroes the glories that had once been Aladdin's, and the Marsh King's, and King Solomon's. . . .

The dark eyes gleamed like a thrush's upon her nest when she is watched.

They saw more mountains, and the cart creeping over them and among them, small as a stone upon the road. And by and by they got down by a brook and began to travel upward towards the source. There were clear and dark pools in the brook where the trout darted and the man with them said: 'The fish runs away, who knows that man has sinned.' They were among steep woods of oak trees as dense almost as grass, all twisted and grey as if made of stone and very old, but based in greenest leaves and flowers of white, of gold, of golden green. The blackbird sang, and the brook gushed, but they did not speak, except that as they left, the strange man said: 'This is the Castle of Leaves.' Now, there was no longer a path, and the way was over whistling dead grass and grey stones, like ruins of a palace that must have been lofty as the heavens, and when they had gone further still the man said it was 'The Castle of the Wind.' And now the mist washed over all and hid everything but silvered stones and dead grass blades underfoot, and the rain that was like bent grass blades of crystal, through which for a moment a sheep crept up and crept away again, or a hare, grey as the grass, but blackened as if by fire, leaped up and dived into the wind, the mist, and the rain. Stumbling still among the ruins of the wind's castle, they continued to climb, until the rocks, now tall as a man and so dense that some had to be scaled, came to an end at the shore of a lake which they surrounded – 'The Shepherd's Lake'. The cry of a raven repeated at intervals from the same spot high up above told them that the mountains rose higher yet and in a precipice. The boy sat upon a rock while the two men went out of sight to the other side; his father to bathe, as he had done twenty years before when a young man. The wind hissed as through closed lips and jagged teeth. The mist wavered over the polished ripples of the lake that resembled a broad and level courtyard of glass among the rough hills. The men were silent, and the sounds of their footsteps were caught up and carried away in the wind. The boy was thoughtless and motionless, with a pleasure that was astonished at itself. He could not have told how long he had been staring at nothing over the lake when, at his feet, his father's head was thrust up laughing out of the water, turned with a swirl, and disappeared again into the mist. He had not ceased to try to disentangle that head from the mist when once more he heard that wailing song that used to make his father so glad, and he himself sang back such words as, without knowing their meaning, he remembered; his brain full of the mists, the mountains, the rivers, the fire in the fern, the castles, the knights, the kings and queens, the mountain boys at cricket, the old man with the foxes, the inn dogs lying in the sun . . . the sun . . . the mist . . . his country . . . not the country he had fought for . . . the country he was going to, up and up and over the mountains, now that he was dying . . . now that he was dead.

Hawthornden

Hawthornden was always home to tea, except once, and it was a significant exception.

When he was about thirty-five Hawthornden moved out into the country, partly because rents were less and he could have a governess for his three children, and so put off for some years the difficulty of choosing a school; and partly, but this was unconsciously, because he had few friends left. As a young man, clever above the common, reckless (within certain limits) and openhanded, he had attracted men of very different types, both at the university and in his bachelor lodgings. But after he married, at twenty-eight, his friends never came to see him, except when they were definitely asked to dinner, though his wife was charming and clever and anxious to meet them, and though he was not too fond of her to attend to them. He seemed to have stiffened and chilled. His smile began to have an awkward catch in it. It was so awkward that it ought to have been dignified, but was not quite. And at the same time as his friends were neglecting him he was not making any progress in domesticity. He had decided against entering a profession, and as he could live on his private means, he was at home very much. But there he gave himself up chiefly to solitary reading, and saw his wife chiefly at meals, and, on evenings when he wished to go early to bed, after dinner. He had thought of writing, but he was squeamish and touchy, and had destroyed his early verses and prose with great care, burning them in his room one summer evening, with a tense, red face, and then, by an after-thought, preserving the ashes in a small cherrywood box. He read many books of almost every kind, except criticism. Criticism he had taught himself to hate, because it seemed to him absurd that the writing class should not only produce books, but circulate its opinion of them among people occupied – like himself – with the business of living at first hand, not at second hand. In the days before criticism life and literature had both been finer things. It was the men with no standards of taste at all who made the arts of the great periods. When there was no one to tell men what to put on their walls, how to build their houses, what to wear and what to read, the glorious things were being created which men instructed at every turn in these matters were content to imitate. Hawthornden sought to recover this freedom by allowing no middleman between art and himself as a human being. As it was, however, physically impossible to keep pace with modern literature without a guide, he neglected it without noticing that this was a concession; and as the old literature had been well sifted by the efforts of the very criticism he despised, he had little left but to enjoy, and he discovered, with some annoyance, that he read and thought – so far as he could express himself – very much like everybody else. Nevertheless, he continued to read abundantly, and for the sake of books put off year by year the problems which his own life offered him. He got out of touch with his wife, ignored her friends, and only by an insincere though determined effort, from time to time, succeeded in quieting her hysteria and relieving her melancholy. As to his children, he made spasmodic and more and more conscious efforts at pleasing and understanding them, and, observing that they could do without him, he plumed himself upon their ingratitude, and left them to the natural methods of his wife, of which he expressed his disapproval from time to time. Yet he was fond of the poetry of passion. He would look up from a poem sometimes and see his wife reading or embroidering, and then take his eyes away with a sigh and only the faintest dissatisfied recognition that he was becoming more and more incapable of being passionate himself and of meeting the passion of another. He also continued to sigh for the simple antique attitudes of the emotions in their liberty, and cursed a time when they could only be seen travestied on the stage. It was literature, nevertheless, and the stage, that had given him the standard which he unconsciously applied to scenes in life which he thought should have been heroical, for example, and were not. Nor was he shaken from his dim-pinnacled citadel of unreality by his one experience of something near tragedy at home. His wife rushed at him one day, with stiff, drawn, red-spotted face and staring eyes, and a shrill voice he had never heard before, to tell him that one of the children was injured. He drew her head to his breast and kissed her hair, and felt at first a kind of shame, then an instinctive disgust at the stains and rude prints of her grief. The same with beauty. He could not have defined it, but he had a standard which he applied to loveliness like a yard-wand, and never suspected that it was the standard that was wanting. It was expression that he feared in living beauty. He wanted the calm of antiquity – of death – of the photographs of celebrated women. A dark face, burning and wrenched with eagerness or delight, disturbed him, and – was not beautiful, because he had been at the trouble of putting aside the expression, and observing that the nose was too small, the eyes unequal, the lips too full, and so on.

He was fond of reading fairy tales and books for and about children, and had acquired strong opinions as to what they needed and liked. He was a great lover of liberty, of liberalism, of freedom for thought and action. He could be heard late at night reading aloud in a deep voice poems on liberty, and even at breakfast would relieve himself by muttering impressively –

> And in thy smile and by thy side
> Saintly Camillus lived and stern Atilius died.

The children looked up and said, 'What did you say, father?' or 'Do say some more like that'; but he stirred his tea, and made haste to leave the table for the study. He admired books of curious character and adventure, such as Borrow's and adored the strange persons who frequented once upon a time, and perhaps even now, the inns and roads of England. He was indignant with civilisation which threatened to extinguish such men, and used to cut from newspapers passages describing the efforts to chain up gypsies and tramps.

When he moved into the country he was prepared for adventures. Gypsies should be allowed to camp near his house and he would be familiar with them. He would invite the tramps into his study for a talk and a smoke. He used to sit by the roadside, or in the taproom of an inn, waiting for what would turn up. But something always stood in the way – himself. He grew tired of paying for a tramp's quart, and was disconcerted, now by too great familiarity and now by too great respect. When a tramp came to the back door, his maids or his wife reported it to him, and they sometimes had interesting fragments of a story to relate; for the women had human sympathies along with unquestioning commonplace views of social distinctions. Sometimes he saw the man coming or going, and formed romantic conjectures which made him impatient of what he actually heard. He thought at one time that perhaps his mistake was in keeping too near home; he would walk far over the hills, and stay away for a night or two. But it was always the same. He dressed negligently and carried a crooked stick, and when he complained of his failure to get at the heart of the wayfaring man, his wife flattered him by saying that any one could see what he really was, whatever his disguise; he liked the flattery, and remained discontented.

Perhaps his whole plan was wrong. He had bought many maps, special walking clothes and boots, compact outfits, several kinds of knapsacks, rucsacs, haversacks, satchels, uncounted walking sticks, just as in other departments of his life he found himself buying pipes suitable for this purpose or that, half a dozen different species of lamps, pens, razors, hats and so on. He tried simplicity for a while, but this also meant a new outlay, and he was soon unfaithful.

Among the people of the neighbourhood he received a reputation for unconventionality. He was said to know the country and the people better than anyone. He was mistaken for a genius, a poet, an artist, a Bohemian, an eccentric millionaire, especially as he had a genuine dislike to parties and picnics and to the sound of men and women trying to put emotion into the words, 'Isn't the weather perfectly glorious?' by drawling them or emphasising one word or each word in turn. He liked the mistake.

But one thing, above all others, gradually disturbed him. He was always home to tea.

He liked a certain kind of tea – the milk or cream of a precise quantity poured out first into his cup and then the tea on top of it, to scald it and produce a colour and flavour otherwise impossible. Then the sweet home-made cakes. . . . Once or twice he went into cottages for tea, to chat with the poor and see them *au naturel*. But he saw nothing, and was therefore keenly alive to the fact that the tea was bad, and the cakes all but uneatable – so that he had a second tea when he arrived home. Mrs Hawthornden was glad of this; she liked him to enjoy himself, and to praise her cakes. She made cakes regularly, and saw that they were of the kinds he preferred. When he started early for a long walk, she used to ask him when he would be back. 'Oh, I cannot possibly say!' he retorted at once; but added, on reconsideration, 'But perhaps by four or five.' He was rarely later than four, and she smiled. He made special efforts not to be back by five – dreading the habit – and yet at last walked so hard as to tire himself in the effort to reach home at that time. So at last, when his wife asked the question, 'When shall I expect you back?' he used to say, sometimes smilingly, sometimes with a submissive despair, sometimes with irritation, 'Oh, I am always home to tea!' When he was not punctual, he was proud – but regretted the cakes – and read Borrow with greater relish. But the next day he would find himself home again to tea, and eating too many cakes with equanimity. He knew they were too many, and the thought at length prevented him from enjoying them, but not quite from eating them; there was a relic of virtue in this inability to enjoy them, though he knew that it might have been greater. At times, in an ancient cathedral or in the midst of a tragic tale, he started with the thought that he was almost forgetting his tea, and then his pleasure was at an end. Lying awake at night, he reproached himself, 'You are always home to tea.' He was haunted by it, as men of noble families of old time were haunted by their fate, and in his moments of complacency it crept suddenly upon him.

One day he went out to a distant part of the county to explore a ruin. It was a fine August day, and he spent most of it in the castle. He left it late in the afternoon, and then began to run. There were several trains that he might have caught; nevertheless, he ran. That day he did not return to tea. His wife looked out a train, and expected him first by one and then by another. It grew dark, and he was not back. The afternoon had been hot, and he had run too fast for a man of his build. He was found lying beside the path. He had achieved his ambition. He had not only not come home to tea, but had ceased to think about tea, so far as can be known. He was dead.

The Artist

This, said Adams to himself, staring strangely at the dry brushes and blank paper before him, this was the fairest day of the whole year, the youngest child of a long family of days, each fairer than its elder. First, there were two days following suddenly, hot and cloudless, upon weeks of storm, of sullenness, and of restless wind and rain vexing the new leaves and scattering the blossoms; and at the end of the second a thunderstorm out of the east ascended lightly and travelled rapidly away without silencing the birds, though the trees were but as reeds in the current of the wildly streaming, visible wind. The night was cloudless, but with few stars. The day after emerged hazy and moaning, but grew slowly into a prime of breadth and splendour without blemish, and sank into a night of steady raining. The next day, and another and a third, were the same, saving that they developed with different rapidity and by unequal stages of mist, breeze, and again mist, before their triumphs of burning brilliance in the sky and joyful multitudinous profusion crowding upon the earth. The nights were misty and troubled over the days which they entombed and cradled. Adams found himself waiting day after day for the end and crown of this energy and change.

There came a lustrous morning early assailed from all quarters of the sky in turn, as if the heavens were besieging the earth, by thunder and after long, brooding intervals, thunder again and again, now with cannonading and now one boom or blast followed by no sound except its echo and the challenge of the pheasants. The lark in the sky, the blackbird in the isolated meadow elms, the nightingale in the hazel and bluebell thickets, sang on; and before the last of the assault Adams set out, inwardly confident in the day's future.

He walked steadily, but more and more slowly, into the broadening and deepening beauty of the great day. So hot was it that the heat alone would have made him happy, and yet the east wind urged him to go on and on. He forgot that it had ever been cold;

it no longer seemed possible that it should ever be cold again; and he was at ease in flesh and spirit, as a creature born for the earth. Now and then he looked at the complicated pale green overflowing the wooded coombes, or at the clouds, stars, or clots of white flowers along the hedges, or at the barley nodding all ways upon already a yard of grey green translucent stalks in the fields above the hollow lanes; and he looked with the calm, experienced, and (he hoped) not jaded eye of an artist turning forty. But, as a rule, if his eye fed it was in pure and independent wantonness, reporting nothing to the brain but pleasure. His eyes did as they listed, wandering or nesting on this hand and that. Adams, in fact, was a heavy and solid body moving through this luxuriant woodland country of deep lanes, gentle hills and short views, for the benefit of those imps and elves, his two eyes. They delighted, as if they had been but ephemeral creatures and not instruments of an immortal soul, in the silkiness and darkness of the long grass, in the towering of one tree, the forking of another, and the inexplicable ramifications of hundreds; in the flight of the swift which was as if the arrow and bow had flown away together. Rarely were his ears allowed a little play, to collect the round notes of the cuckoo, the raptures of the nightingales, the calm, easy fluting of the blackbirds.

But satiated with the earth of morning, noon, and afternoon, his eyes tended more and more to the sky. There in the north were clouds, farther away than he had ever before seen clouds, the most delicate of toppling marble mountains, grey-white with a glistening white profile towards the sun, and midway between him and these were a few long, thin strands of a dark blue-grey lying horizontally. Round about the sun itself hung a mass of this blue-grey, edged with fiery gold; and at times that mass disappeared, leaving the sun – as if all that cloud were the fuel of its fury – a dazzling white conflagration filling a quarter of the sky. He walked as if he were going to walk into the heavens beyond the hills.

Again, his eyes fell to the earth. For the first time in the day they dwelt on human faces. It was in a short village street ending at a churchyard, a street of uniform old brick cottages with flat fronts right upon the roadway – all but one, and that had a tiny bow window which seemed all glass. In this window a white-haired woman stood talking to a dark girl, looking straight at her with eyes and lips together, while the girl's eyes, somewhat abased, looked out on to the street. Adams saw chiefly her white dress and her dark eyes, because they were fixed on him and even followed him, yet without the least curiosity or understanding. 'Little and brown and lovely is my love,' were the words of his thought as he passed by, but he did not know whether they were remembered or inspired. It was a good group, quite apart from the fact that the girl was beautiful.

    Past the church, only just out of the sound of the sermon, Adams sat on a gate. The wind had gone away, perhaps up into the sky to comb out the white clouds into curled fleeces; the air below was still as thought. Lowering his head, he saw nothing nor thought of anything, so far as he knew, for an unmeasured space of time. Suddenly a noise of many cattle running in the field behind drew his eyes that way. They had disturbed whatever was going on in his head, and he got down and was almost past the gateway when he glanced once more into the field, and saw white on the other side of it – a girl in white – certainly the girl who had stood in the bay window. A youth in black was leaning beside her over a gate, and stroking some cart-horses. She very soon grew impatient, and for a time stood with her back to them, though they snuffed her hair. But seeing that her companion took no notice, she raised the arm nearer to him and caught his, and tried, without any physical effort, to draw him away from the gate, that they might walk on. At that moment she seemed to Adams to be a little older than her lover, twenty perhaps, while he could not have been more than eighteen. He did not move. Then she took one step away still holding his arm, and with her eyes upon his face, but in vain. So she slid her hand down to his, and made another step away, and a second, still looking up at him; and thus their two arms were now fully stretched out. At the end of the field, several windows, under white-edged gables, looked at them out of the vicarage, from which they had probably come. The youth felt their gaze; for her, the house might have been swallowed in the earth, the earth itself might have been swallowed up, without troubling her eyes or her heart. Only when she bent her head and kissed his imprisoned hand did he face her and give way, and begin slowly to walk alongside of her from the gate. The horses thrust their heads far out, and he turned round; he would have gone back, had she not taken his hand in both of hers, bending as she did so and fastening her eyes upon his, and, as she thought, upon his soul; whereupon he threw up his arms suddenly, and sent the animals racing away.

All her movements were beautiful. By the side of the stiff youth in black she was like a wave lapping at a rock. Adams stood quite still, watching her through the sprays of hawthorn at the edge of his gateway. He had grown happy and breathless in her beauty, and yet sad to see her actions as of one who had given all to one who had not and could not. It was her lover's dog that had set the cattle running, and when it did so again his shout of command was clear, hard, and controlled. She, Adams knew, could not have shouted so. She was strong, spirited, and without fear, but she was too gentle, he thought. Her yielding gestures were still imperious, and the two were now walking slowly and close-linked – she smiling as she took strides equal to his – but in a few days, in a year. . . . Yet Adams drew some lines upon paper to remind him of her body bent and head raised when she clasped her lover's hand in both of hers. He watched them receding, and did not take his eyes off them until they had rounded a corner and passed wholly out of sight.

Starting at length to continue his walk, he looked at the sketch abstractedly. He was not a great or even a much-praised artist; he was not a vain man; yet suddenly came into his mind an entirely unforeseen and unfamiliar thought – 'Perhaps these pencil marks will endure until after those two lovers are old and after I am dust.' He sighed involuntarily, and immediately smiled self-consciously at the absurdity and apparent vanity of the thought. Then, while his mind was occupied he knew not where, with a grave look he tore the paper into many pieces, and dropped them into the ditch, so that they should not disfigure the grass.

The Attempt

Several seasons had passed since Morgan Traheron had so much as looked at his fishing tackle, and now he turned over, almost indifferently, the reels and lines and hooks and flies which had been carefully put away in an old tool box of his great-grandfather's. He looked at the name 'Morgan Traheron' cut neatly inside the lid, and shivered slightly during the thought that one of his own name had bought it in 1776 at the ironmonger's and brazier's under the sign of the 'Anchor and Key' near Charing Cross, and that the owner had been dead nearly a hundred years. Cold, cold, must he be! Even as cold would be the younger bearer of that name, and he anticipated, in a kind of swoon, the hundred years that would one day submerge himself from all known friendliness of sun, earth, and man.

He was seeking, not any of the fishing tackle, but a revolver that lay amongst it, and a small green box containing only one ball cartridge. He had often thought of throwing the revolver away. His wife always looked wonderingly at him when he cleaned it once every year or so, but if she had urged him to throw it away he would have scoffed at the fear which he detected, all the more heartily because the sign of her concern inflated his vanity. She, lest she should provoke his mood in some way which even her consideration could not foresee, remained silent or asked him to tell again how he shot the woodpigeon fifty yards off, actually within sight of the gamekeeper's cottage. It was a thrilling and well-told tale, albeit untrue.

It was not a mere accident that one ball cartridge was left.

Morgan took out the revolver and the cartridge and shut the box. The lock was stiff and the chambers would not revolve without the use of both hands. To fire it off, it would therefore be necessary to twist the loaded chamber laboriously round to its place and then force back the hammer to full cock. The barrel was brown from rust, but probably the ball would force its way through as it had done before. It was a cheap, ugly, repulsive weapon; it impressed him with unsuitableness. He did not stay to oil it, but putting it in a pocket and the cartridge in another, he prepared to leave the house.

'Won't you take Mary with you, Morgan?' said his wife.

'Yes,' said Mary, his little daughter, laughing not so much because there was anything to laugh at as because she must either laugh or cry, and certainly the chance of a walk was nothing to cry for: 'Take me with you, father.'

'Oh no, you don't really want to come, you only say it to please me,' said Traheron, mild but hard.

'Yes, I am sure she . . . Good-bye, then,' said his wife.

'Good-bye,' said he.

The thought of kissing his daughter turned him back for a moment. But he did not; the act occurred to him more as a part of the ceremony of this fatal day than as a farewell, and he feared to betray his thought. She was the immediate cause of his decision. He had spoken resentfully to her for some fault which he noticed chiefly because it disturbed his melancholy repose; she had then burst out crying with long, clear wails that pierced him with self-hate, remorse, regret, and bitter memory.

Why should he live who had the power to draw such a cry from that sweet mouth? So he used to ask in the luxurious self-contempt which he practised. He would delay no more. He had thought before of cutting himself off from the power to injure his child and the mother of his child. But they would suffer; also, what a rough edge would be left to his life, inevitable in any case, perhaps, but not lightly to be chosen. On the other hand, he could not believe that they would ever be more unhappy than they often were now; at least, the greater poverty which his death would probably cause could not well increase their unhappiness; and settled misery or a lower plane of happiness was surely preferable to a state of faltering hope at the edge of abysses such as he often opened for them. To leave them and not die, since the child might forget him and he would miss many a passing joy with her, was never a tolerable thought; such a plan had none of the gloss of heroism and the kind of superficial ceremoniousness which was unconsciously much to his taste. But on this day the arguments for and against a fatal act did not weigh with him. He was called to death.

He was called to death, but hardly to an act which could procure it. Death he had never feared or understood; he feared very much the pain and the fear that would awake with it. He had never in his life seen a dead human body or come in any way near death. Death was an idea tinged with poetry in his mind – a kingly thing which was once only at any man's call. After it came annihilation. To escape from the difficulty of life, from the need of deliberating on it, from the hopeless search for something that would make it possible for him to go on living like anybody else without questioning, he was eager to hide himself away in annihilation, just as, when a child, he hid himself in the folds of his mother's dress or her warm bosom, where he could shut out everything save the bright patterns floating on the gloom under his closed eyelids. There was also an element of vanity in his project; he was going to punish himself and in a manner so extreme that he was inclined to be exalted by the feeling that he was now about to convince the world he had suffered exceedingly. He had thus taken up the revolver, and blurred the moment of the report by thinking intently of the pure annihilation which he desired. The revolver was the only accessible weapon that entered his mind, and he had armed himself with it without once having performed in thought what he had committed himself to do in fact before long.

As he mounted the hill by a white path over the turf, he felt the revolver strike against his hip at each stride. He was in full view of anyone who happened to be looking out from his home, and he pressed on lest the wavering of his mind should be seen. Recalling the repulsiveness of the weapon, the idea of a rope crossed his mind, not because it was preferable, but because it was something else, something apart from his plans which now had a painful air of simplicity.

When he was among some bushes that concealed him and yet still gave him a view of his house, he paused for breath. He half-longed for an invasion of sentiment at the sight of his home; but he was looking at it like a casual stranger, and without even the pang that comes when the stranger sees a quiet house embowered in green against which its smoke rises like a prayer, and he imagines that he could be happy there as he has not until now been happy anywhere. The house was mere stones, nothing, dead. He half wished that Mary would run out into the garden and compel him to a passionate state. His will and power of action were ebbing yet lower in his lifeless mood. He moved his eyes from the house to the elder hedgerow round it, to the little woods on the undulations beyond, to the Downs, and, above them, the cloudy sun perched upon a tripod of pale beams. Nothing answered his heartless call for help. He needed some tenderness to be born, a transfigured last look to keep as a memory; perhaps he still hoped that this answer that was not given to him could save him from the enemy at his side and in his brain; even so late did he continue to desire the conversion, the climacteric ecstasy by which life might solve its difficulty, and either sway placidly in harbour or set out with joy for the open sea.

He mounted the upper slopes and passed in among the beeches. He turned again, but again in vain. There was little in him left to kill when he reached the top and began to think where exactly he should go. He wished that he could hide away for ever in one of the many utterly secret mossy places known to him among beech and yew in the forsaken woods; the foxhounds might find him, but no one else. But he must go farther. The sound of the discharge must not be heard in that house below. Almost with tenderness he dreamed of the very moment when his wife would hear the news and perhaps see his body at the same time; if only that could be put off – the announcement must not come to-day, not under this sun in which the world was looking as he had always seen it, though more dull and grey, but on some day he had not known, a black, blind day yet unborn, to be still-born because of this event so important to him. Who would find him? He did not like the thought that some stranger who knew him by sight, who had never spoken to him, should come across the body, what was left of him, his remains, and should suddenly become curious and interested, perhaps slightly vain of the remarkable discovery. If only he could fade away rapidly. Several strangers with whose faces he was familiar passed him in a lane, and he assumed a proud, hard look of confidence, as he hoped.

He quickened his steps and turned into a neglected footpath where he had never met anybody. He took out the revolver and again looked at it. It was just here that he had come in the hottest of the late summer to show his daughter cinnabar caterpillars, tigerish yellow and black, among the flaming blossoms of ragwort. The ragwort was dead now, blossom and leaf. He recalled the day without comment.

He was now hidden, on one side by a dense wood, on the other by the steep slope of a hill, and before and behind by windings of the path which skirted the wood. He inserted the cartridge and with difficulty forced it into position; the brass was much tarnished. Now he revolved the chambers in order that the cartridge should be under the hammer, but by mistake he turned them too far; he had to try again, and, losing count of the chambers, was again defeated. Where the cartridge was he could not be sure, and he looked to see; its tarnished disc was hostile and grim to his eye, and he hid the weapon.

Moving on, he now looked down upon a steep wood that sloped from his feet, and then rose as steeply up an opposite hill. They were beech woods with innumerable straight stems of bare branchwork that was purple in the mass. Yews stood as black islands in the woods, and they and the briers with scarlet hips close to his eye were laced with airy traveller's joy, plumy and grey.

Traheron now turned the muzzle to his temple, first letting the hammer down for fear of an accident. He had only one shot to fire, and he could not feel sure that this would enter his brain. His ear, his mouth – the thought was horrible, impossible. His skin ached with the touch of the steel which was very cold. Next he turned the weapon to his breast, and saw that he had better pull the trigger with his thumb. The hammer was now at full cock, the cartridge in place. The hideous engine looked absurdly powerful for his purpose. The noise, the wound, would be out of proportion to the little spark of life that was so willing, so eager, to be extinguished. He lowered the weapon and took a last sight of the woods, praying no prayer, thinking no thought, perfectly at ease, though a little cold from inaction.

Suddenly his eye was aware of someone moving above the opposite wood, half a mile away, and at the same moment this stranger raised a loud halloo as if he had sighted a fox, and repeated it again and again for his own delight, feeling glad, and knowing himself alone. Traheron had been watching the wood with soul more and more enchanted by the soft colour, the coldness, the repose. The cry rescued him; with shame at the thought that he might have been watched, he raised the revolver and turned it to his breast, shut his eyes and touched the trigger, but too lightly, and breathless, in the same moment, he averted the barrel and hurled it into the wood, where it struck a bough without exploding. For a moment he dreamed that he had succeeded. He saw the man who found him pick up the revolver and examine it. Finding but one cartridge in the chambers he concluded that the dead man was a person of unusual coolness and confidence, with an accurate knowledge of the position of the heart. Then, for he was cold, Traheron moved rapidly away, his mind empty of all thought except that he would go to a certain wood and then strike over the fields, following a route that would bring him home in the gentleness of evening.

He opened the door. The table was spread for tea. His wife, divining all, said:

'Shall I make tea?'

'Please,' he replied, thinking himself impenetrably masked.

Morgan

The storm is over; Morgan is dead. Once more we can hear the brook's noise, which was obliterated all night by the storm and by our thoughts. The air is clear and gentle in the forest and all but still, after the night of wind and of death. High up in the drifting rose of dawn the multitudes of tall, slender trees are swaying their tips, as if stirred rather by memory of the tempest. They make no sound with the trembling of their slender length: some will never sound any more, for they lie motionless and prone in the underwood, or hang slanting among neighbour branches where they fell in last night's storm, and the mice may nibble at crests that once wavered among the stars. The path is strewn with broken branches and innumerable twigs.

The silence is so great that we can hear, by enchantment of the ears, the storm that passed away with night. The tragic repose of ruin is unbroken. One robin sings, and calls up the roars and tumults that had had to cease utterly before his small voice could gain this power of peculiar sweetness and awe, and make itself heard.

The mountains and sky, beautiful as they are, are more beautiful because a cloak of terror has been lifted from them and left them free to the dark and silver, and now rosy, dawn. The masses of the battlemented mountains are still heavy and sombre, but their ridges bite sharply into the sky, and the uttermost peaks are born again. They are dark with shadows of clouds of a most lustrous whiteness that hang, round above round, like a white forest, very far off, in the country of the sun, and the edges of the rounds are gilded; seen out of the clear gloom of the wood, this country is as a place to which a man might wholly and vainly desire to go, knowing that he would be at rest only there. In the valley between this forest and the mountains the frost is rosy with the roses of the zenith.

As we listen, walking the ledge between precipice and precipice in the forest, the silence seems to murmur of the departed tempest like a sea-shell, and we also remember again the sound of the dark hills convulsed with a hollow roaring as of an endless explosion.

Trees were caught up and shaken in the furious air like grasses; branches were stricken and struck back, were ground and beaten together and broken. The sound of one twig was drowned by that of myriads; the sound of one tree by that of leagues; and all were mingled with the sound of the struggle in the high spaces of the air. Between earth and sky there was nothing but sound and darkness plunging confused. Outside the window branches were brandished wildly, and their anger was the more terrible because the voice of it could not be heard or distinguished amidst the universal voice. The sky itself seemed to aid the roar. It was dark with the darkness of black water, and the planets raced over it among floes of white cloud; dark, menacing clouds flitted on messages of darkness across the white. We looked out from the death-room, having turned away from the helpless, tranquil bed and the still wife, and saw the forest surging under the wild moon, but it was strange and no longer to be recognized while the earth was heaving and be-nightmared by the storm. Yes, the forest is still under the awe of that hour. That is why its clearness is so solemn, its silence so pregnant, its gentleness so sublime. But not for that only. It is fresh after the sick room, calm after the storm and after the vain conflict with death, sad because every thought in it leads to death, and made majestic by the character of the life that has ended and never saw this dawn. It is as if his soul had bereaved the forest also. The robin's song is poured into the silence and shivers and is chilled by falling into the dark cave of death, as a brooklet falls over a cliff into a sunless sea.

The blue smoke rises straight up as if nothing had happened from the house of death, over there among the white fields. As if nothing had happened! But we have been walking here an hour, and have come to see even in that smoke a significant tranquillity as of a beacon or sacrifice. It comes from the room where the wife sits and looks at the white face peering through its black hair like seaweed, and still speaking of the old ecstasy, solitude, and irony that it had in life. A strange life – of which the woman who shared without breaking his solitude can tell nothing, and would tell nothing if she could: for she wishes only to persuade us that, in spite of his extraordinary life, he was a good man and very good to her. She has become as silent as he is and as he was. Nevertheless, they say that twenty years ago, when she began to live with him on the mountain, she was a happy, gay woman, the best singer and dancer in the village, and had the most lovers, while now her wholly black, small Silurian eyes have turned inwards and have taught her lips their mystery and Morgan's, have taught also that animal softness to her steps and all her motions. It would not be surprising were she to strive to be buried along with him, if only she had not lost so much of herself in losing him. She guards him like a hound and like a spirit. She shadowed and clung to the doctor and the minister, so that their offices were a mockery, yet they dared not attempt to keep her away. Perhaps she will go back to his Tower and live there alone.

If this winding path between two of the forest precipices be followed to that bank where the eastern sun now falls upon the dazzle of a myriad celandines, the top of Morgan's Tower, or Folly, can be seen against a wedge of sky among the hills; there are no trees at that height, and it is distinct and unmistakable. It is a slender, square tower containing three rooms one above the other, and above these an uncovered look-out. If she returns there she will be able to visit the upper room and the look-out for the first time.

Morgan built the Tower before he was thirty, and he dwelt there nearly thirty years; whether out of cruel constancy to his first resolution, no one knows; but once he had gone there he never left it, except to die in the great house where he was born, and where he chiefly lived, until the building of the Tower. For a time he tried to live entirely in London, devoting himself and his riches to social reform, which seemed the only way to gain some tranquillity and save himself from too often remembering that he was in hell. He drew back because he could not understand the town life, and it was absurd to reform what he could not understand. At first, and for several years, the sight of the men and women and children living a pure and simple town life allowed him no rest. It was easy to provide them with things which seemed to him to be good for them. But it was not easy, it was in the end not possible, to put away the thought that his motive was a false one, and yet one for which he could see no practical alternative. He was trying to alter the conditions of other men's lives because he could not have endured them himself, because it would have been unpleasant to him to be like them in their hideous pleasure, hideous suffering, hideous indifference. He saw in this attitude a modern Pharisaism, whose followers desired not merely to be unlike others, but to make others like themselves. It was due to lack of imagination, he thought, of imagination which would enable the looker-on to see their lives as compared with their conscious or unconscious ideals. Did they, for example, fall farther short from their ideals than he from his? He had not the imagination to see, but he thought perhaps not; and he did see that, lacking as their life might be in antique beauty and power, it yet had in it a profound unconsciousness and dark strength which might some day bring forth beauty – might even now be beautiful to simple and true eyes – and had already given them a fitness to their place, such as he himself was far from having reached. He never hesitated when it was food and warmth that were lacking, but beyond supplying those needs he could never feel sure that he was not fancifully interfering with a force which he did not understand and could not overestimate. So leaving all save a little of his money to be used for giving food and warmth to the hungry and the cold, he escaped from the sublime unintelligible scene. He went up into the Tower, that he had built upon a rock in his own mountains, to think about life before he began to live. Up there he hoped to learn why it was that sometimes, in the London streets, beneath the new and the multitudinous there was a simple and pure beauty, beneath the turmoil a placidity, beneath the noise a silence which he longed to reach and to drink deeply and to perpetuate, but in vain. He desired to learn to see in human life, as we see in the life of bees, the unity which perhaps some higher order of living beings can easily see through the complexity that confuses us. He had set out to seek at first by means of science, but he found that science was only the modern method of looking at the world, possibly a transitory method, and that too often it was an end and not a means. For a hundred years men had been reading science and experimenting, as they had been reading history, with the result that they knew – some science and some history. So he went up into his bright Tower.

    From there he looked out at the huge, desolate heaves of the grey beacons. Their magnitude and pure form gave him hours of great calm. Here there was nothing human, gentle, disturbing, as in the vales. There was nothing but the hills and the silence that was God. The greater heights, set free from night and mist, looked as if straight from the hands of God, as if here He also delighted in pure form and magnitude that was worthy of His love; and the huge shadows moving slowly over the grey spaces of winter, the olive spaces of summer, were as His hand. While Morgan watched, the dream came, more and more often, of a paradise to be established upon the mountains when at last the sweet winds should blow across a clean world that knew not the taint of life any more than of death, and then his thought swept rejoicing through the high Gate of the Winds that cleft the hills far off, where a shadow ten miles long slept across the peaks, but left the lower wild as yellow in the sunlight as corn. Following his thought he walked upward to that Gate of the Winds, to range the high spaces, sometimes to sleep there. Or he lay among the gorse – he could have lain on his back a thousand years hearing the cuckoo among the gorse and looking up at the blue sky above the mountains. Or in the rain and wind he sat against one of the rocks among the autumn bracken until the sheep surrounded him, half visible and shaggy in the mist, peering at him fearlessly as if they had not seen a man since the cairns were heaped on the summit; he sat on and on in the mystery, part of it but divining it not, and in the end went discontented away. The crags stared at him on the hill-top, where the dark spirits of the earth had crept out of their abysses into the day, and still clad in darkness looked grimly at him, at the sky, and the light. More and more he stayed in his Tower, since even in his own mountains, as in the cities of men, he was dismayed by numbers, by variety, by the grotesque, by the thousand gods demanding idolatry instead of the One whom he desired, Whose hand's shadow he had seen far off. Looking on a May midnight at Algol rising out of the mountain, the awe and the glory of that first step into the broad heaven exalted him; a sound arose as of the whole of time making a music behind him, a music of something passing away to leave him alone in the silence, as if he also were stepping up into the blue air – always to stumble back. Or it was the moon rising. Then the sombre ranges to eastward seemed to be the edge of the earth, and as the globe ascended the world was emptied and grieved, having given birth to this mighty child; he was left alone, and the great white clouds sat round about upon the horizon and judged him. For days he would lie desolate and awake and dream and stir not. Once again he returned to London and saw the city pillared, above the shadowy abyss of the river, on columns of light; and it was less than one of his dreams. It was winter and he was resolved to work, and was crossing one of the bridges, full of purpose and thought, going against the tide of the crowd. But the beauty of the bridge and the water took hold of him. It was a morning with a low, yellow sky of fog. About the heads of the crowd swayed a few gulls, interlacing so that they could not be counted, and they swayed like falling snow and screamed. They brought light on their long wings, as down below a great ship setting out slowly with misty masts brought light to the green and leaden river upon the foam at her bows. And ever about the determined careless faces of the men swayed the pale wings like wraiths of evil and good calling, and calling to ears which do not know that they hear. And they tempted his brain with the temptation of their beauty; he went to and fro to hear and see them until they slept and the crowd had flowed away. He thought that they had made ready his brain, and that on the mountains he would find fulness of beauty at last, and simplicity, so he went away and never returned. There, too, among the mountains was weariness, because he also was there.

But not always weariness. For was not the company of planet and star in the heavens the same as had bent over prophet and poet and philosopher? By day a scene unfolded, as when the first man spread forth his eyes and saw more than his soul knew. These things lifted up his heart, so that the voices of fear and doubt were not so much in that infinite silence as little rivers in an unbounded plain. There were days when it seemed to him the sheer mountains were the creation of his lean, terrible thoughts, and he was glad, and the soft, wooded hills below and behind were the creation of the pampered luxurious thoughts he had left behind in the world of many men. It was thus, in the style of the mountains, he would have thought and spoken – but language, except to genius and simple men, was but a paraphrase, dissipating and dissolving the forms of passion and thought. Then, again, time lured him back out of eternity, and he believed that he longed to die, as he lay and watched the sky at sunset, inlaid with swart forest, and watched it with a dull eye and a cold heart.

So much was known or could be guessed from his talk. For in those early days of his retreat he was not silent to those who met him upon the mountains, nor did he turn aside so as not to encounter them. And much more was told in the legend that flourished about the strange truth, and at last entangled and stifled it, so that the legend was all, and no one cared about the man. He was said to have buried money somewhere in the caves of the hills. He was said to worship a God who had never entered chapel or church. He was said to speak with raven and kite and curlew and fox. He was said to pray for the end of man and the world. He was called atheist, blasphemer, outlaw, madman, brute. But the last that was known of him was that one summer he used to come down night after night courting Angharad who became his wife. One of the most persistently reported of his solitary obsessions was the belief in a race who had kept themselves apart from the rest of men though found in many nations, perhaps in all. Some said the belief was from the Bible and that this was the race that grew up alongside the family of Cain, the guiltless 'daughters of men' from whom the fratricide's children took their wives. These knew not the sin or the knowledge or the shame of Adam, Eve, and Cain – so he was said to believe – and neither had they any souls. They were a careless and godless race, knowing neither evil nor good. They had never been cast out of Eden. Some of the branches of this race had perished already by men's hands, such as the fairies, the nymphs, the fauns. Others had adopted for safety many of men's ways, and had become moorland and mountain men, living at peace with their neighbours and yet not recognized as equals. They were even to be found in the towns. There the uncommon beauty of the women sometimes led to unions of violent happiness and of calamity, and now and then to the birth of a poet or musician or a woman who could abide neither with the strange race nor with the children of Adam. They were allowed to live and compelled to suffer for their power and beauty. Their happiness – it was considered by men to be something other than happiness, lighter, not earned or deserved, mere gaiety – was the cause of envy and hate, and it met with lust or with torture. They were feared, but more often despised, because they retained what was charming in the animal with the form of men, and because they lived as if time was not, and yet could not be persuaded to a belief in a future life. Up in his Tower, Morgan came to regard his father as one of these, the man who had forsaken his wife before the child was born, and left only a portrait behind. If only he could capture one of this race, thought Morgan, and make her his wife, he would be content. And Angharad, the shy and bold and fierce and dark Angharad, whose black eyes radiated light and blackness together, was one of them. So he took her up to his Tower.

After that these things only were certainly known: that she was unhappy; that when she came down to the village for food she was silent, would never betray him or fail to return; and that he never came down, that he also was silent, that he looked like a wild man with unshorn hair. He was seen at all hours, always far off, on the high paths of the mountains. His hair was as black as when he was a boy. He was never known to have ailed, until one day, the wild wife knocked at the door of his birthplace, and asked for help to bring him where he might be tended as was necessary, since he would have no one but her in the Tower. And so he came and last night he died, having thanked the Earth for its strength and its beauty, for what it had given him and for what it might have given had he been wise, having prayed that his body might be dutiful to Earth in the grave and bound up more purely than it had been during his living days 'in the bundle of life with the Lord my God.' She has not always been silent, but has cried aloud with a voice far wilder than the curlew's because she is left alone with the children of men. And that is why this gentle morning is so grave and so forlorn, and why Morgan's Folly stands up so greatly and notably in its blackness against this dawn.

(1913)

The Ship of Swallows

SOMEONE was talking in very glowing words about a sunrise, and this set the artist raging:

'Hark at that gentleman talking about a sunrise – in October, too – and his only one, I warrant! Half our modern verses and prose for that matter would never have been written if an unwonted early rising or late sitting had not set the writer's nerves on edge, and made their nasty vapours "stream in the firmament." This Nature poetry-stuff is the jejune enthusiasm of townsmen who are ashamed to confess that they are such. It dates from the turning of England into a town with a green backyard. When men lived in the fields and rose early, they cared too much for these things to think to please one another by writing impressively about them. Who of these men, or of outdoor men to-day, can stomach fellows like that arum-lily talking, and the poet he quotes, who at least has the wisdom to watch his dawns from a comfortable bed?'

The speaker was a little wiry man, with blue eyes in a brown tangly face like speedwells in a furze bush, whose fondness for being about at all hours of the day and night was extreme enough to explain the low repute of his canvases.

'But you go too far the other way,' said a mild, pale man with spectacles, whose body was bent in a slight curve by his large head. 'The dawn has always been the same. . . .'

'I deny that,' said the youngest. 'The dawn changes as men change. Caractacus would not recognize a dawn of Turner's, and I should only be interested as a person with an historic sense in the kind of dawn that lighted Caractacus to his spear and his sword.'

'The dawn,' continued the mild, pale man, 'has always been the same, and clothes the passing of time for us, in spite of our clocks, as for those who had none, with beauty and awe. It will be some years before a man ceases to feel himself a member of no mortal or only mundane commonwealth, when he sees with what ceremony the day begins. At this hour Nature wears the buskin, and justifies all poetry and pride of man. I see chiefly sunsets myself. It does not suit me to rise for sunrises in town when I am working, or in the country when I am trying not to work. Still, I have seen them. My father farmed two hundred and fifty acres in Kent, milked forty cows, and grew enough hops to make half a hundred children happy for a week in picking them. . . . No, well, I don't pretend to be a countryman, except while I am rheumaticky.'

The artist was smiling good-naturedly now. He liked the stiffly-curved man in spite of a certain stateliness. The two took a turn round the garden together. The artist was lured so far as to talk about dawns simply for what weather they foretold. The other went on:

'The beauty of a dawn in fair weather does me good. I believe it liberalises my feelings for the rest of the day. In spite of ill health I think I may say I have no morbidity. I have heard women speak as if they felt just what I feel, and they have less morbidity and less poetry than men. But I remember one in particular, chiefly because of the extraordinary unsought image by which it is now represented in my mind. You might do a painting of it, though it is more suitable for a symbolist.

'We lost our second child when she was only a year old. She died in the afternoon, in the middle of a shower that suddenly dashed down upon the heat of July. Soon after midnight my wife at last fell asleep. I could not sleep. So I put on my clothes and read a book, a story or two of very thin stuff as it seemed to me, and I have never cared for that author since. I put down the book and went out. Very soon I left the streets and walked with the edge of the common on one side, and on the other the gardens of some old-fashioned houses now demolished. There had been no more rain, and there was no wind. There was no sky visible. The air thickened into a downy grey, motionless, and without either stars or forms of cloud. A clock tinkled three. There was just a pallor in the darkness. The dawn was thinly and evenly poured into every inch of air between earth and sky. The night was dying, but instead of day replacing it, a neutral, soft grey was succeeding that might be the end and dissolution of all; as if all things were melted down in this cup of grey air; and this idea was at the time not unpleasant. Some big trees overhung a little cottage at one side of my path. All their million leaves were still.

The Ship of Swallows 77

'I was tired, and I leaned upon the gate. A thrush began to sing very clear. On the other side of the common another sang, and a third and perhaps a fourth farther away. There were not so many as in May, yet enough to mingle into a strange pleasing little medley. I knew that if I could have travelled at that hour from there to my father's house, there would be thrushes all the way, in gardens, in roadside trees, in hedges and thickets.

'I did not see them fly up, but presently two swallows were twittering on the chimney of the cottage. It was not the musical, happy twitter of sunlight, but lower and perhaps timid: they did not yet dare to launch themselves into the air for the day's flight. It was sound, nevertheless, that prevented me from thinking of anything else – I was very tired, you must remember. I did not notice the thrushes any longer whilst listening to this low twitter. It was as soft and pallid as the light, and increased with it in quality very slowly. I was now leaning back and looking at nothing but the whitening grey sky. I do not think I closed my eyes, but I found myself looking up at the bows of a huge, dark ship, very high, and overhanging me, and gleaming as if with dew. It rose up shadowy, and I could not see the bulwarks. I cannot tell how I knew that it was a ship, though I could see portions of a figurehead, a woman's breast and throat and head leaning forward. But it was a ship, and it was just setting out on a voyage, as it seemed to me, of peculiar solemnity and significance, like that of Columbus or St Brendan or Jason; even the sea before it – though it stood upon the grassy land – was infinite and mysterious. Clinging about the ship's sides were many swallows, hardly visible against the gleaming black timber, but sharply outlined upon the white and gold of the figurehead. They were twittering low with clustering, sweet notes. There was awe at the sea and the solemn voyage in the sound of their little voices. There was expectation also, and a sort of blind, gentle hope. And I knew that I was to go on board of that ship soon, and to share in the mystery and the hope. When I opened my eyes the light was beautiful, though the sun was not up in the gilt sky. The swallows were still twittering, but they were flying now backwards and forwards over the garden and along the roadway. The feeling of expectation and hope remained, and a subdued cheerfulness that must have had something to do with the tranquillity of those next few days with all their gloom. . . .'

A THIRD-CLASS CARRIAGE

WHEN the five silent travellers saw the colonel coming into their compartment, all but the little girl looked about in alarm to make sure that it was a mere third-class carriage. His expression, which actually meant a doubt, whether it was not perhaps a fourth-class carriage, had deceived them; and one by one – some with hypocritical, delaying mock-unconsciousness, others with faint meaning looks – they began to look straight before them again, except while they cast casual eyes on the groups waving or turning away from the departing train. Even then every one looked round suddenly because the colonel knocked the ashes out of his pipe with four sharp strokes on the seat. He himself was looking neither to the right nor to the left. But he was not, therefore, looking up or down or in front of him; he was restraining his eyes from exercise, well knowing that nothing worthy of them was within range. The country outside was ordinary downland, the people beside him were but human beings.

Having knocked out the ashes, he used his eyes. He was admiring the pipe – without animation, even sternly – but undoubtedly admiring what he and the nature of things had made of the briar in 1910 and 1911. It had been choice from the beginning, not too big, not too small, neither too long nor too short, neither heavy nor slim; absolutely straight, in no way fanciful, not pretentious; the grain of the wood uniform – a freckled or 'bird's-eye' grain – all over. In his eyes it was faultless, yet not austerely perfect; for it won his affection as well as his admiration by its 'cobby' quality, inclining to be shorter and thicker than the perfect one which he had never yet possessed save in dreams. A woman who by unprompted intelligence saw the merit of this favourite could have done anything with the colonel; but no woman ever did, though when instructed by him they all assented in undiscriminating warmth produced by indifference to the pipe and veneration for its master. As for the men, he had chosen his friends too well for there to be one among them who could not appreciate the beauty of the pipe, the exquisitely trained understanding of the colonel.

He was not merely its purchaser; in fact, it was not yet paid for. The two years of expectant respect, developing into esteem, cordial admiration, complacent satisfaction, had not been a period of indolent possession. Never once had he failed in alert regard for the little briar, never overheated it, never omitted to let it rest when smoked out, never dropped it or left it about among the profane, never put into it any but the tobacco which now, after many years, he thought the best, the only, mixture. Its dark chestnut with an amber overgleam was reward enough.

As he filled the pipe he allowed his eyes to alight on it with a kindliness well on this side of discretion, yet unmistakable once the narrow but subtle range of his emotional displays had been gauged. He showed no haste as he kept his pale, short second finger working by a fine blend of instinct and of culture; his whole body and spirit had for the time being committed themselves to that second finger-tip. After having folded the old but well-cared-for pouch, removed the last speck of tobacco from his hands, and restored the pipe to his teeth, he lit a wooden match slowly and unerringly, and sucked with decreasing force until the weed was deeply, evenly afire. The hand holding the match, the muscles of the face working, the eyes blinking slightly, the neck bending – all seemed made by divine providence for the pipe.

When the match was thrown out of the window, and the first perfect smoke-cloud floated about the compartment, only the eye that sees not and the nose that smells not could deny that it was worth while. The dry, bittersweet aroma – the perfumed soul of brindled tawniness – was entirely worthy of the pipe. No wonder that the man had consecrated himself to this service. To preserve and advance that gleam on the briar, to keep burning that Arabian sweetness, was hardly less than a vestal ministry.

There was not a sound in the carriage except the colonel's husky, mellow breathing. His grey face wrinkled by its office, his stiff white moustache of hairs like quills, his quiet eyes, his black billycock hat, his unoccupied recumbent hands, the white waterproof on which they lay, his spotless brown shoes matching the pipe, were parts of the delicate engine fashioning this aroma. Certainly they performed no other labour. His limbs moved not; his eyes did not see the men and women or the child, or the basketful of wild roses in her lap, which she looked at when she was not staring out at the long, straight-backed green hill in full sunlight, the junipers dappling the steep slope, and whatever was visible to her amongst them. His brain subdued itself lest by its working it should modify the joys of palate and nostrils.

At the next station a pink youth in a white waterproof, brown shoes, and hollycock hat, carrying golf-clubs and a suit-case, entered the carriage. The colonel noted the fact, and continued smoking. Not long afterwards the train stopped at the edge of a wood where a thrush was singing, calling out very loud, clear things in his language over and over again. In this pause the other passengers were temporarily not content to look at the colonel and speculate on the cost of his tobacco, his white waterproof, and his teeth and gold plate, on how his wife was dressed, whether any of his daughters had run away from him, why he travelled third-class; they looked out of the window and even spoke shyly about the thrush, the reason of the stop, their destination. Suddenly, when all was silent, the little girl held up her roses towards the colonel saying:

'Smell.'

The colonel, who was beginning to realize that he was more than half-way through his pipe, made an indescribable joyless gesture designed to persuade the child that he was really delighted with the suggestion, although he said nothing, and did nothing else to prove it. No relative or friend was with her, so again she said:

'Smell. I mean it, really.'

Fortunately, at this moment the colonel's eyes fell on the pink youth, and he said:

'Is Borely much of a place, sir?'

Every one was listening.

'No, sir; I don't think so. The railway works are there, but nothing else, I believe.'

'I thought so,' said the colonel, replacing his pipe in his mouth and his mind in its repose. Every one was satisfied. The train whistled, frightening the thrush, and moved on again. Until it came to the end of the journey the only sound in the carriage was the Colonel knocking out the ashes of his pipe with a sigh.

The Pilgrim

The 'Dark Lane' is the final half-mile of a Pilgrim's Way to St David's. It may be seen turning out of the Cardiganshire coast road a little north of the city. Presently it crosses the 'Roman road' to Whitesand Bay, and then goes down into the little quiet valley that holds the cathedral and a farm and a mill or two. Travel has hollowed out this descent; bramble and furze bushes on the banks help to darken it. Yet the name of 'Dark Lane' is due rather to the sense of its ancientness than to an extremity of shade. Perhaps on account of the shadow it may cast on the spirits of men it is now little used, unless by the winter rains; and some days of storm had made it more a river than a road when I walked up it, away from St David's. I looked back once or twice at the valley, its brook – the Alan – its cathedral, and the geese on its rushy and stony pasture. I had no conscious thought of antiquity, or of anything older than the wet green money-wort leaves on the stone of the banks beside me, or the points of gorse blossom, or a jackdaw's laughter in the keen air. If the pilgrims never entered my mind, neither did living people. The lane itself, just for what it was, absorbed and quieted me.

I was therefore disturbed when suddenly, among the gorse bushes, I saw a young man kneeling on the ground, his back turned towards me. If he had not heard me approaching he knew, as soon as I stopped, that some one was there. He was more surprised and far more disturbed than I. For in a flash I had seen what he was kneeling for; and he knew it. He was cutting a cross on a piece of rock which had been left uncovered by money-wort. Obviously he felt that I must think it odd employment for him on that December day.

He was not a workman carving a sign or a boundary stone, or anything of that sort. He was nothing like a workman, but was clearly a young man on a walk. A knapsack and a thick stick lay at his side. He was dressed in clothes of a rough homespun, dark sandy in colour, good, and the better for wear, and with nothing remarkable about them except that the coat was not divided and buttoned down the front, but made to put on over his head. As he wore breeches he showed a sufficient pair of rather long legs. His head was bare, and his brown hair was untidy, and longer than is considered necessary for whatever purposes hair may be supposed to serve. He might have been twenty-five, and I put him down as perhaps a poet of a kind, who made a living out of prose.

He looked at me with his proud, helpless, blue eyes; his lips moving with unspoken words. He shut the knife he had been using as a chisel, and opened it again. I knew that he would have given anything for me to go on after saying 'Good morning,' but I did not go. I asked him how far it was to Llanrhian, and if the main road beyond here was the original continuation of the 'Dark Lane', or if part of it was missing, and so on. He answered, probably, by no means as best he could, for he was thinking hard about himself. In a few minutes he could no longer keep himself to himself, but began to talk.

'I suppose you wonder what I was doing, cutting that cross?' he said in a defensive tone.

'Was there an old pilgrim's cross there?' I asked innocently. 'I have heard they carved crosses on some of the stones along the road.'

'I have heard so too,' said he; 'but I have been looking out for them all the way from Cardigan and have not found any.'

'Then you have carved this yourself?'

'Yes; and I suppose you wonder why. Well, I don't know; I can't tell you; I don't suppose you would understand; I am not sure if I do myself; and at any rate it is no good now.'

'I hope my interrupting you . . .'

'Oh, no, I don't think so. But when I began I thought it would be a good thing. I got as far as this at daybreak, and I was feeling . . . what is it to you? Seeing this old stone, which is perhaps the last before I reach the cathedral, and no cross on it any more than on the others, an idea came to me. I had been thinking about those pilgrims, some of them with torn feet, some hungry, or old, or friendless, or with an incurable disease. And yet they came here to St David's shrine. They must have thought there was some good in doing so; they would be better, even though their feet might still be torn, or they might still be old, or hungry, or friendless, or have their incurable disease. But the shrine is now empty.

I did think that perhaps the place where the relics used to be, when they were not carried out to battle, would have some power. All that faith would have given it some quality above common stone. But I doubted. Then I thought. "But faith is the thing. If those pilgrims had faith there was no special good in St David's bones, except, again, that they believed there was." I tried to think in what spirit one of them would have carved a cross. Perhaps just as a boy cuts his name or whatever it may be on a bridge, thinking about anything or nothing all the time, or sucking at a pebble to quench his thirst. At the sight of this stone – I may have been a fool – I thought – I had a feeling that while I was doing as the pilgrims did I might become like one of them. So I threw off my knapsack and chiselled away. . . . Please don't apologize. In any case it would have been no good. The knife was already too blunt, and I was cold and aching and also thinking of a wretched poem. Do you think a pilgrim ever had such thoughts? If there was such a one he would never have got far on his road.'

I tried hard to lure him into a Socratic dialogue to disclose what had brought him so far. He went on:

'The quickest city in the world is St Pierre, which was overwhelmed by the volcano on Mont Pelée. But one cannot easily become a citizen of St Pierre. Well, well, what is it to you that I want in some way to be better than I am? I must be born again: that is certain. So far as it is in my power, I have tried hard. For example, there is no ordinary food or drink or article of clothing I have not given up at some time, and no extraordinary one that I have not adopted. There remains only to wear a silk hat and to drink beer for breakfast.

'I have been to physicians, surgeons, and enchanters, but they all want to know what is the matter with me. I answer that I came to them to find out. Then they listen gravely while I tell them about a hundredth part of the outline of my life. They write out prescriptions; they order me to eat more or eat less, or to be very careful in every way, or not to worry about anything. They shake hands, saying: "I was just like you when I was your age. You will be all right before long. Good-bye."

'My family paid a specialist to come to see me at the house once. He and I had the usual conversation. Then he was given lunch, which he ate in complete silence, except for a complaint about the steak. After receiving his cheque my mother asked him rather tragically what to do. "Don't hurry him on, Mrs Jones," he said, "and don't keep him back, Mrs Jones."

'For forty days I visited an enchanter continually. He did not promise to cure me, though he also said that at my age he was just like me – which was untrue, for he had a Yorkshire accent. Day after day in his room I sat with closed eyes, repeating "Lycidas" silently with the object of not thinking about anything, especially the incantation. This consisted of a whispered, slightly hesitating assertion that I should get well, that I should be happy, that I should have faith, that I should have no more doubt, but confidence, concentration, self-control, and good sleep. After several minutes I always heard the enchanter take out his watch to see if he had given me enough. From that time until the end I was doing little but listening to the crackle of his shirt-front and cuffs. It was so funny that I was even more serious about it than he; but after forty days I had had enough. My rebirth did not take place in the house of the enchanter.'

'When I was your age . . .' I began; but luckily I was inaudible.

'I have tried many medicines,' he continued. 'I have been to a physician who offers to cure men who are suffering from many medicines. All in vain. I tried a medicine which all great writers take, and which presumably makes them greater or keeps them great; but it had no effect on me – my literary ambition died.'

Here he took out his watch.

'Zeus!' he said. 'I have been two hours at this thing,' and he rose up. 'I must photograph that cross and put it in my book. That will pay for the wasted time.'

He photographed the stone and cross, and departed with long strides down the 'Dark Lane' before I could ask about his book, but I see no reason to doubt that he was writing a book.

The Friend of the Blackbird

For the whole of one year, whenever my daily walks led me down a certain old lane that used to be full of sun and forgetfulness, I was sure not to have it to myself. It was no longer used as a road, the farm it had served once being covered up in ivy and nettle; and as a footpath it was not a short cut to anywhere. Until that year I had met no one there. I have not met anyone there since. He was nearly always in the same place, just where the first bend in the lane shut out the road. At first, I thought he looked unusually out of place, with his new, stiff clothes, tall grey hat, polished ebony walking-stick, and movements angular and precise. I was not glad to see him – an invalid, I supposed – in a place which I once believed to be my own, and could not regard as a thoroughfare.

One day he stopped me by asking the name of a flower which he pointed out tenderly and politely with his glossy stick. As he spoke he turned his eyes towards me, though hardly upon me, so that I seemed to be bathed in their light, which had a cold brightness and purity as of newly melted frost, and a blissfulness also which was so intense as to be unearthly. Clearly he was one who saw invisible things. Feeling that he was not looking at me I could observe his eyes closely, and they were indifferent to my curiosity. They were moistly bright, of a clear grey, and almost circular, the lids being unnoticeable under the gentle arches of thick, light-brown eyebrows; their expression was of childlike earnestness and simplicity, tinged with surprise that might almost have been fear. His face was square, and the delicate skin, drawn tightly over prominent bones, was nearly all concealed by the short brown hair on cheeks, lips, and chin. Through the hair showed a pair of lips matching the eyes – full, moist, shapely, and soft, of an unblemished innocence. He was short, squarely but lightly made. His voice was in keeping with eyes and lips; it was deep, slow, and soft almost to a breaking point.

I saw him many times before we spoke more than a few words again. As I passed he used to cast upon me that bright, unchanging glance without any kindliness in its gentleness, and seemed to feel rather than to see that I was on that common plane where everybody knows what you mean because you mean nothing in particular. In reply I could only look upon him with curiosity that was quickly overcome by discomfort, by awe, and even a kind of dread. Beauty, genius, or happiness, each in its own way, compels awe akin to fear, in the detached beholder. This man had happiness. Never before or since have I seen happiness so shining. Where at first I had blindly seen only his external incongruity with the untended hawthorns and virgin grass, I came to see perfect fitness. He was entirely at home there. In my memory the intensity of his happiness is all the more wondrous because of the pain of his end not much more than a year after I saw him first.

 He knew himself that he was to die soon.

 He was the son of a farmer among the mountains. When he had to go to school at eight or nine years old, it was in a town within sight of the ridges, but thirty miles away. In the town he had grown up. He was there when his father died, and except on the day of the funeral he never revisited his home. Tired of school, he left of his own accord and became a collier. For six days out of seven he washed only his lips clean, and that with ale. At the end of the sixth he washed the whole of his face, that he might kiss a maid. He fell in love. But the maid died, and at her funeral he dropped, fainting, into the grave. From that day he began to read all night. He seldom saw the sun, except on Sundays, and then only through the windows of his bedroom where he worked, or of his chapel. He began to preach, and in a few years was thought fit to be a minister. His furious pieties in the pulpit won him at first a congregation that would travel many mountain leagues on horseback or on foot to hear him. But out of the pulpit he was a different man. He was silent and morose. He would take no part in festivals, in music, in politics, in judgments of erring man or woman. They thought him proud; they muttered that they would not go on paying a man to mount up into the clouds for one day in the week, and when he had recovered from a long illness, he found he must go to a small house in the hills to serve two chapels many miles apart. He had loved God overmuch. But he did not cease from loving. God hid Himself from this worshipper, but he kneeled and smiled as if God had loved him. He thought of no one else; there was none but Him and of Him he thought as winter changed to spring, and spring to summer, and summer to winter, as roads glide into one another. He did not look down to behold the earth and sea, nor up to the sky. There was nothing for him but God, and the two little grey chapels far from man, on the great moors.

Once again he fell ill and in his delirium the truth passed before his eyes – that he had loved God overmuch and His creatures too little. Sickness left him unable to walk any more from chapel to chapel over the cloudy hills. He had to teach little children in a hamlet so poor that they were glad of him. There he lived alone, except for the children and the birds that inhabit the lean oaks of the stony copses, the alders along the brooks, the fern upon the lone crag that filled half of his northern sky. Since his illness he had forgotten about God, and remembered only the misery of his creatures. But the children and the birds cheered and taught him. On this earth he learned that it was a man's part to love the earth and its children. There would be plenty of time left in eternity for loving God. We do not demand, he reflected, that the maidservant lighting a fire at dawn should think about the sun, or that the soldier loading his rifle should think about his king; and so an earthly man need not greatly be troubled about anything but his fellow-men and animals, companions of the brief lifetime that is as a meadow in one of the folds of the mountain of eternity. In those old days, he thought, when the Lord went over Jordan with the children of Israel, men were as children, and He walked with them, but now He has ascended and we see Him not until we also shall have gone up, we know not whither. Nor did his thought perish when another sickness overthrew him and left him one hand trembling as if it were no longer his own. The children presented him with the ebony stick, and he left them to die. In the meantime he had taken to this lane.

Sometimes he brought a book out with him, and when he did, it was a book of travel or natural history. He had an inexhaustible desire to know about everything that lives on the earth, both near and far. He had learned the songs of many birds, and spoke of them familiarly with admiration and delight. The immensity and variety of Nature, as he found himself, or read of it in the gorgeous records of travellers, were a source of continual satisfaction; he had never dreamed of them before. Everywhere he found beauty, personality, and differences without end. The old simplicity and horror of the world conceived as the abode of evil man and a dissatisfied, incompatible Deity were forgotten. He could speak of God without emotion. After reading a book in which a liberal and gentle soul created a liberal and gentle Deity, and showed the necessity for his own adherence to the religion of his fathers, his only comment was: 'It is a good book . . . a good God, but not a very great God after all . . . What does that thrush say? We must consider him. But so far they do not seem to know very much about him, except his skeleton and his diet. There must be one God for both of us. We can afford to wait. So can He.' But that was only a casual, light-hearted expression of the creed that was coming to him under the sky. He turned away to look at a blackcap singing every minute high up in golden-green blossom against the blue sky, where the sun and the south-west wind ruled over large, eager grey clouds with edges of gleaming white. The little dead-leaf coloured bird quivered all over; his throat swelled in bubble after bubble; his lifted black head was turned from side to side as he sang; and he moved slowly among the blossom.

The high, quick, dewy notes filled the paralytic with a thin, exquisite pleasure, as if his soul had climbed upon the line of his vision and crept into the singing bird. 'All these things are mine. They are me. And that is not all: I am them. We are one. We are organs and instruments of one another.' He did not forget the trees – 'those tethered dreamers, standing on one leg like Indian mystics.' With them also he felt the same community, as though more rarely and in a way not to be spoken except by putting out his hand to touch their bark and leaves. The animals, too, were more remote than the birds, and reminded him too often of men's careless sins of cruelty. He did not preach kindness to animals, but pitied those men who had not yet awakened to the need of kindness, as if they must be suffering for the lack as much as the animals. He could not tell why men kept birds in cages to sing. Their freedom in living and dying was lovely to him. Every creature, including man, is best in freedom, he said, looking up at the white clouds coursing in the freedom that was from everlasting to everlasting. He sighed with regret, mingled with apology, as animals slipped away out of sight. Then he was glad to hear the blackbird and thrush again, the sweet, lively talking of the thrush and the pure melody of the blackbird. They were his favourites. He could talk of the different blackbirds he had known, and their places in town or wild, and describe their differences. With a little laugh, because he remembered the days before he had such thoughts, he said plainly that they had souls and lived, as we do, after death, though he did not know, nor perhaps did they, what life it might be. Only, there was one thing in the blackbird that he could not enjoy – probably, he admitted, because he could not understand; and that was the laughing, discordant notes that often concluded his song, especially in the late spring. This distressed him, partly because it was not musically in keeping with the song, and partly because the bird seemed to be laughing at himself. He had been reading Byron, and it reminded him of the way the poet sometimes wound up a stanza with a cynic phrase; and he could not enjoy this in bird or poet. Those birds were children of the sun, he said to himself. Before, if not above, all birds and all creatures, he loved the sun. The only time when he mentioned again the little grey chapel that stood highest among the mountains was to conjecture that it was built near the site of a temple for sun-worship. There were large upright stones in an adjoining field that were said to have formed part of a sun temple; and he liked to remember that. It was the God, not of the old stones, but of the chapel, that descended upon him in his last illness.

For weeks he lay sick and wild with dreams of the night and fears of the day. He raged and accused himself of unpardonable heresies, and defiance alternated with remorse. He was placid only while he whistled over and over again with unearthly sweetness and clearness, a fragment of one of the mountain songs of the blackbird, heard far away in the wild lands. It was a fantastic whim, for Whatever overpowered him in that friendless death-chamber, amid snow and silence, to wrest such blasting discords out of an instrument that had seemed in the lane to know only natural joy and tranquillity. 'The little God,' he said, in one of his latest moments of relief, 'the little God torments me.' And again: 'But I go to the Great One. It is well.'

Friend of the blackbird, is it well?

The Land of Youth

The last of the heroes left in Ireland was Ossian, the greatest of the warriors who were also bards. He was a son of Finn, but lived on into Patrick's time and would sit talking to the saint and even listening to him. The saint had sprinkled holy water on the hero, yet for a little while he was not sure that he ought to be talking to such a one except about Christianity, of which Ossian was too old to know anything. But two angels answered his doubts. They told him that he should write down the words of Ossian, especially his tales of the times of old, because they would give gladness to after times.

Ossian was now as gentle as any Christian. He could not ride, or run, or sing clear, but most of his time sat leaning forward on his spear, like some old apple-tree that has lost all but one of its branches and has long borne no fruit save pearls of mistletoe. He belonged to a race whose deeds and stature and way of life seemed more fitting to the earth than Christian men's, more in harmony with mountains, forests, stormy seas, and heavens. He would listen to tales of religion, but it was impossible to make him a Christian; he was altogether too old and gigantic, and his memory was too full. When Patrick or some duller priest tried to stir him by saying that Finn and his brothers and companions were not in Heaven, he replied: 'If they be not there, what should I do there? Why should I go there?' He was never tired of describing the godlike Finn. When a priest told him that not even a midge could slip into Heaven without God's knowledge, he recalled the generosity and hospitality of Finn. If the leaves of autumn were gold, he said, and the sea waves silver, Finn would have given all away. Thousands of men could enter his hall, feast at his board, and leave without being questioned. The heroes, he said, used to speak truth and keep their promise as well as any priest. Patrick stood looking at him, his head not much above the end of the bloodstains on Ossian's spear. He would have been willing that all men should be giants if they had been as noble as the sons of Finn. He knew little men who were far more monstrous.

Whatever a priest said, Ossian was too old and mild to be often sad, except when the wind was from the east. Then the long and cold nights wearied him, and he remembered the chase and the warfare with the long-haired sons of Finn. He knew then that he could no longer hunt, or fight, or play, or swim in the torrents, that he was a poor old man without strength or music. He was left alone on the earth, and would have been glad to be with Finn his father and Oscar his son, wherever they were. It still irked him that he had not been there to aid his father in the battle when every inch of the great Finn was stretched cold and still beside the Boyne. Nor did he share the last battle of the Fena, when Oscar slew Cairbre and died himself, and only the swift-footed one of the tribe escaped. It was his own fault that Ossian had missed these battles. Strange it was that such an adventure of youth should have been the means of drawing out his life to so great an age! He told Patrick the tale.

On a misty spring morning Finn and the Fena, and Ossian among them, were hunting among the Lakes of Killarney. They were in full chase when they were suddenly aware of a single rider galloping on a white horse towards them. The stag and the hounds ran on, but all men stopped to see the beautiful woman riding out of the West. She reined in the horse a little way from the motionless hunters. Her eyes had the blue of the dewdrop reflecting a cloudless sky; her cheeks were crimsoned white like snow at dawn; her curled golden hair concealed the diadem and rings of gold which were meant to adorn it. She wore a mantle of brown precious silk, golden-starred and clasped with a brooch of gold, flowing down over the red-golden saddle and the white horsecloth to the gold hooves and the green grass. She was slender and her white hand small, yet she rode the galloper with more grace than the swans rode the water. 'I have ridden,' she said, 'from a far country.'

Finn asked her name and country, and she said she was Niav of the Golden Hair, daughter of the King of Tirnanoge, beyond the west sea. She had come because she could love no other man but the high-spirited and famous Ossian, son of Finn. When Ossian heard her pronounce his name he loved her. As she governed the great horse with her little hand, so she governed him from that time with a sweet voice that sounded strangely among the company of hunters. Whatever her voice said he was bound to love Niav, but presently she began to utter things that might have made the voice of the jay seem sweet. For when Ossian had spoken his love and given her a true gentle welcome to his country, she said:

'Thou must come with me on my horse to Tirnanoge, the Land of Youth. It is the loveliest and most famous country under the sun. Leaf, blossom and fruit cover the trees at one time and for ever. Gold, silver and all that delights the eyes, abound there. It flows with wine and honey. Thou shalt have there a hundred swiftest steeds, a hundred perfect hounds. Thou shalt have a coat of impenetrable mail and a sword that cannot be resisted or escaped. Thou shalt have jewels not of this world. Thy herds shall be without number. Thy flocks shall have golden fleeces. Each day shall be one of feasting and harp-playing. A hundred warriors in full armour and a hundred harpers with sweetest music shall be at thy call. Thou shalt wear the diadem of the king of Tirnanoge, which no other but he ever wore, and it shall preserve thee from all perils of day and night. Thou shalt have beauty and strength everlastingly. Decline shall never come to thee, and thou shalt not know decay or death, and I shall be thy wife in Tirnanoge.'

Finn and the Fena burst out into lamentation when they saw Ossian turning towards that maiden and towards the West. Finn took his hand and said:

'Alas, my son, thou art going away, and I fear thou wilt not return.'

Though Ossian said: 'After a little I will come back to see thee,' his father did not stop weeping as they embraced, nor yet when he mounted the white horse behind Niav. They galloped away westward, smoothly and swiftly to the sea-shore. They spoke not a word, because Niav had said, 'Let us be silent until we reach the sea.' The only sound was the mourning of Finn and the Fena.

Shaking himself and neighing three times as he touched the water, the horse raced forward as if the waves had been grass. He was swifter than a March wind on the mountain-tops. Now on this hand and now on that the riders saw strange coasts of islands and continents, with cities and white palaces and strong places shining on the green land above the water. They were far out beyond the course of ships, but once a hornless fawn tripped beside them, running before a white hound with red ears; and they saw a lovely maiden, on a brown steed, carrying a golden apple, and following her a young warrior on a white steed, clad in a mantle of crimson satin, and bearing a golden-hilted sword. Ossian asked who were the riders.

'There is nothing in these things,' said Niav, 'they are nothing compared with the marvels of Tirnanoge.'

They rode on until they saw in the farthest distance a sunny palace above the waves, and Ossian asked whose palace it was and who was the prince.

'It is the Land of Virtues,' said Niav, 'ruled over by the giant Fomor. His queen is the daughter of the King of the Land of Life. He carried her away by force and keeps her by force in the palace, where she waits for a champion to fight the giant. No man has been found of great enough courage.'

'I,' said Ossian, 'will be her champion and rescue the Queen.'

The beautiful young queen welcomed them and gave them chairs of gold, choice food, golden goblets of wine and mead; and Ossian promised to be her champion, to kill the giant or to be killed in the attempt. The giant approached, ugly and huge, bearing a great bar of iron for a club, and without bowing or saluting, offered to fight Ossian. For three days they fought; and Niav and the Queen stood by weeping. At last Ossian struck down the giant, and as he lay smote off his head. For a minute there seemed two giants instead of one, the gnarled head rolling its eyes and thrusting its tongue between its fangs, and the mountainous heaving body. Niav and the Queen raised a cry of joy at the sight. They led Ossian into the palace and washed and healed his wounds, and when he was restored he covered up the hideousness of Fomor under a cairn.

'It was a lovely land,' said Ossian to Patrick, 'and if Heaven hath equal glories I should praise your God.'

Nevertheless the lovers parted from the Queen, who was as sorry for their going as she was glad of her release. They rode on towards Tirnanoge. Once more their course was over the sea. They saw the hound following the fawn, and the young warrior after the maiden carrying the golden apple. A storm arose, but not foam above or waves beneath troubled their course. In the brightness of lightning and in the after blackness they rode on happily and as quiet as the fish at the bottom of the deep. When the sun conquered they saw before them a land of flowers and long lawns, lakes and rivers shining, with chains of cataracts and high blue hills. Between the strand of gold and the hills rose a palace adorned with carving and overlaid with gold and many-coloured stones, and Niav said:

'This is Tirnanoge.'

A company of warriors came down from the Palace to meet them. After them followed the King of Tirnanoge in a crown of diamonds and gold and a garment of bright gold, and with him the queen and her maidens, and a host glittering with arms and armour and sounding with the music of harps, and in the intervals the blowing of trumpets. The king took Ossian's hand and welcomed him before the host and led him into the palace. There they feasted for ten days and celebrated the marriage of Ossian and Niav.

Tirnanoge was as beautiful and happy as Niav had said. Her words, indeed, even with the accompaniment of her lovely voice, falling on a lover's ears, had represented the beauty and happiness of the country only as words can do to those who have not seen what they describe. It was more pleasant to Ossian to enjoy than it was afterwards bitter to remember. So many were its pleasures that when he recalled his life there a hundred things were forgotten, and yet it seemed impossible. For Tirnanoge had made young his soul and body. The battles of old which he had fought in Ireland, the wounds, the weariness, the anxiety, the mourning, no longer helped to stiffen his limbs and weigh down his heart. He rose up in the morning glad and he lay down at night content. He was never tired of doing pleasant things many times over. Each present hour was as happy to him as the long-past hour seems to men who have never been in Tirnanoge. Seldom did the old days in Ireland return to his mind. When they did he saw the heroes and their fights, all as beautiful and quiet as the pictures upon the walls. Thus he saw the mild, wise, generous Finn his father in many acts of his life, but above all on the day when he struck his dog Bran. The noble dog looked at him in wonder, and as Finn stooped to make up for the blow by a caress, he wished that the arm had been torn from his shoulder before it had offended. He saw the sweet-tongued bard, his uncle Fergus; his own mighty son Oscar, who won back a lost battle with a tree trunk for weapon; the one-eyed Gaul; the beautiful, chivalrous Dermat. He saw them in chase and battle, always triumphing by their truth-telling and the might of their hands. He recalled the trial-days for men seeking to join the ranks of the Fena. The candidate was bound never to refuse hospitality, never to insult a woman, to take no dowry with his wife. Having promised these things, he was tested for strength and courage. He had to stand in a pit exposed from the knees upward, and with only a shield and a hazel wand to turn aside the spears hurled at him by nine warriors together. Also he was given a short start and had to race through the forest before armed men: he could shelter himself only by tree trunks, but if wounded or caught – if even he had broken a branch in his course or unbraided his hair, or if his weapons at the end trembled in his hands – he could not become one of the Fena. He had to run at full speed and without slackening pluck a thorn out of his heel, jump a branch as high as himself, and stoop under one no higher than his knee.

His memory showed him these things, and they were curious and amusing. He did not know that they were memories. They belonged to a life so unlike that of Tirnanoge, that he saw them without knowing that he himself had once hunted with those hunters and warred beside those warriors. He laughed at some of them as at outlandish scenes. The life of Tirnanoge was all beautiful, being of a kind that men have always refused to think possible, because it was active and full of variety yet never brought death or decay, weariness or regret. This cannot easily be imagined by earthly men. They say that perfect happiness would be dull if it were possible. If they could imagine it, they would not love it so utterly when they possessed it like Ossian; many would refuse it because it wipes out the desire and the conscious memory of earth. The men of Tirnanoge remember earth without knowing what it is they are remembering, just as in dreams we may recall what we did not know had ever happened to us.

For hundreds of years Ossian lived with Niav in this forgetfulness. They had three children, two sons and a daughter, and they called the sons Finn and Oscar. But one day as he was hunting he saw an eagle. He closed his eyes and he saw the bird still, but in a different scene. It floated above a mountain that ended in a red precipice and a lake below. He saw not one lake but several, one beyond the other, among the mountains, and upon one a swan floated. Instantly the swan made him think of Niav. In this there was nothing strange. But he thought of her not as she was then, but as she was when he first saw her riding in Killarney, and he saw with equal clearness the warriors bidding him farewell as they had done three hundred years ago. This was memory, and Ossian knew it. Very old and rude and shaggy they looked, like a clump of trees upon a hill-top, and he longed to ride straight away to Killarney. But his heart was troubled. He felt that he could not trust his horse to run upon the waters, so he rode home to Niav and told her and the king that he wished to visit Ireland. They said they would not stop him, but Niav said:

'I fear, Ossian, thou wilt not come back again, once thou hast returned to Ireland. Ireland is not what it was. Finn and the Fena are there no more. Saints and priests are in their places. Yet I fear thou wilt not come back. Thou must not touch the soil of Ireland with thy feet. Thou never canst come back if thou dismount from the white horse and touch Irish earth. Never canst thou see me or I see thee again if thou forget this.'

Ossian wept but he rode away towards Ireland, passing again the islands and continents and cities and palaces. When he reached Ireland he seemed to see nothing that he knew. The smell was the same, some of the distant mountains also. But the Fena were not there. He saw what looked like men far off, but having ridden up to them he saw that they were not; for they reached only to the gold clasp in his instep. They were kind and courteous and they spoke Irish, but they looked up and wondered. He questioned them about Finn and Oscar and the rest.

'We have heard of Finn,' they said. 'He was a wise and generous king in Ireland once upon a time. The poets tell of him and his companions. There were great men in those days and the Fena were great amongst them. The poets sing of them. Finn, they say, is dead long ago, and his brothers and sons and grandsons and companions are all dead. They were great men, heroes taller than we, every one of them as tall as yourself, but they are all dead of their wounds. All except one, as the poets say. He was one of the sons of Finn named Ossian. He left his father and all that company to go with a maiden to Tirnanoge. He said that he would come back, but he never did. They sought him, but before they could find him they were dead. But for the poets they would be forgotten. . . .'

'Poets?' said Ossian, in sorrow and in anger. 'What poets can there be if Fergus be dead and Ossian in Tirnanoge?'

His heart was too heavy to be long angry with these little images of men. He turned away his horse and rode on to the well-known places of battle and hunt and feast. Finn's palace was the home of winds and birds above, of chickweeds and nettles below. The cooking places of the Fena still scarred the high moors, but the heroes were gone. No men had seen them. They could only show him writings containing the names of Finn, Ossian, Fergus, Oscar, Gaul, Dermat, and the rest. Wherever he went he heard about these poems instead of the champions. Men stared at him, but none guessed he was Ossian, one of the Fena. Hither and thither he rode visiting all the scenes of the Fena's exploits. But he saw only the little creatures made in the image of men. He felt very pitiful towards them.

One day in the Glen of Thrushes he saw a cluster of these men trying to lift up a huge stone. They were three hundred, but they could neither raise it to its place nor get free from underneath it, and they said:

'O kingly champion, help us.'

So Ossian stretched himself forward upon his horse's neck and stooped and gripped the stone in one hand. All the little men ran out from underneath like lizards disturbed. Then Ossian put forth his strength. He raised the stone above his head and threw it. It covered the multitude like a high roof as it flew. But he had burst the saddle girth of his horse with the effort; the saddle slipped and he could not recover himself; and his feet touched the earth. The white horse vanished away. Now came altogether the change and decay that could not befall him in Tirnanoge; his strength ebbed away fast, and he sank sighing down like a wave; he became the old, frail, mighty one who leaned on his spear and would listen to Patrick talking about Heaven, and would talk to him of Niav and of Tirnanoge, the Land of Youth.

The Making of the Worlds, of Gods, and of Giants

Long ago, in Iceland, there was a king named Gangler who was famous for wisdom and for magic, and there were few things which he could not understand. One thing alone always astonished him, and that was the fact that whatever the Gods willed came to pass. He did not know whether this was due to their own great wisdom or to that of some even mightier Gods whom perhaps they themselves worshipped as men did them. This question returned to his mind again and again, even when he was old.

One day while the king was thinking about this power of the Gods he rode far away from his palace without looking at the road, and leaving his horse, which was a new one, to take him wherever it pleased. For he was thinking very hard. He did not know even that he was hungry. He did not know that what he was seeing was not the things around him, but those in his own brain. He was thinking about the Gods and their palace of Asgard, and he could see them as plain as his own warriors and his own house; in fact the Gods were very much like his warriors, and the palace of Asgard very much like his house, except that they were larger and looked as if they must last for ever. It was not until the horse stumbled that he saw anything else but Gods and Asgard. He slid gently off on to the ground, and the young horse, glad to be free, walked on, turned round, and galloped away.

As Gangler followed the horse with an indifferent eye he saw that he was far up on the side of a stony mountain. It seemed as huge as the sky, especially as the pale stones scattered about it resembled the flocks of white clouds when those flocks are at their smallest and highest in the blue. Though he had never before been on this mountain or any like it, he was in no way surprised or alarmed. It was, in fact, just such a mountain as he had been seeing with his mind's eye for some time. At the top of it was a palace such as he imagined the Gods' palace of Asgard to be. With untired step he went on up the slope towards it. It did not seem to him a wonderful thing that he should have come in this short time to Asgard.

The first thing he saw was a mansion huge as a hill, roofed with golden shields instead of tiles; and a man stood at the entrance tossing up and catching seven swords to amuse himself.

'What is your name?' said the man. 'Gangler,' said he; 'I have come a long way and should be glad of a night's lodging. Pray tell me whose house this is.' 'It is the king's,' said the man, and led him into the hall. He saw room after room, and many people in them, some drinking, some at play, others fighting. He went without fear, yet very carefully, through the crowd, from room to room, until he came to one where he saw three thrones one above the other, and three crowned men like brothers sitting on the thrones. 'Who are these?' asked Gangler. 'The one on the lowest throne is a king, and his name is Har; the second is equal to him, and is called Jafnhar; the highest is Thridi, and he also is a king.' Now Har himself spoke to Gangler, asking his errand and telling him that all strangers were welcome to eat and drink in his hall. 'But first,' said Gangler, 'I should be glad to know if there is any one here famous for wisdom.' Har smiled: 'Unless you show yourself the wisest, O man, I fear you may not return in safety. Stand below, and here sits one who will be able to answer your questions.'

Gangler bent down before the lowest of the thrones and began to ask his questions.

'Who is the first or eldest of the Gods?' he asked.

'All-Father,' answered Har, in a voice like thunder, 'but he has twelve names.'

'Where is this God? What is his power, and what are his works?'

'He has been from the beginning,' answered Har, 'he reigns everywhere: all things obey him.'

And Jafnhar said in a voice like the sea: 'He made heaven and earth and air, and all that dwells in them.'

Thridi also spoke, and his voice was like wind in the forest: 'He made man, and gave him a soul that cannot die.'

'But where,' asked Gangler, 'where was this God before he made heaven and earth and air?'

'He was with the Frost Giants,' said Har.

'And what was before that?' continued Gangler.

'In the beginning,' said Har, 'there was no earth, no sea, and no heavens. There was no grass; there was nothing but a yawning chasm such as no man can imagine and such as would make the Gods dizzy even to think of.'

'Long before the earth,' said Jafnhar, 'a cloud world was made, called Niflheim, a cold world of everlasting fog, rain, and sleet.'

At these words Gangler felt himself upon a ship, as once he was in his younger days, sailing over an unknown sea after a storm. He saw before him the dim rocks and the dim marshland on the shore of an island where he could find no men, and nothing alive but sea-birds all crying together as they flew round about in the mist. It was between a wet autumn and a bitter winter. The coast of that uninhabited island seen through the sea-spray, the mist, and the low grey clouds must have been like Niflheim. He remembered yet another scene. He had just stepped out of his house after a night of rain and wind. The rain and the wind had beaten round the walls all night, so that as he lay awake, the only man awake in his hall, he seemed to be on a ship. And as he stepped out in the morning he thought at first that he was in the middle of the sea. Below him was the steep hill on the top of which stood his house, but the hill was blotted out by mist. Through the mist he could see mountains which he had never seen before, but either they, or he and the house, were moving. He dared not take another step lest he should fall into that strange sea. Then as he stood still thinking, he saw that the mountains were clouds. His house and the little piece of ground where he was standing seemed to be all that was left of the earth. The night's storm had washed away all the rest, and there he was shipwrecked in a sea of clouds and mist, rocking and swirling round about. This sea must have been like Niflheim.

'But before Niflheim,' said Thridi, not noticing Gangler, 'there was a world in the south called Muspellheim. It is a flaming and burning world, too bright and too hot for any one, man or god, who was not born there. It is guarded by one with a flaming sword seated at its border. His name is Surtur, and at the end of the world he will go forth with his flaming sword and harry and overcome the Gods and burn the world.'

'Tell me more,' said Gangler, 'of the chasm between this burning world and Niflheim.'

Thridi answered him: 'One half of the chasm was fog and frost from Niflheim, the other bright because of the sparks and flakes of fire of Muspellheim; and in the middle part the frost was melted and the drops of the vapour rising from it grew into the shape of a man. This was Ymir, the ancestor of all the Frost Giants.'

'Where did he live?' asked Gangler, 'and how did he live?'

'A cow also was made out of the drops of the melted frost,' said Har, 'and four rivers of milk flowed from her teats, and Ymir lived on the milk.'

'What did the cow feed on?'

'The cow fed on the salty hoar-frost that she licked from the stones. At the end of the first day hair like a man's appeared on the stone that she had licked; at the end of the second there was a man's head; on the third the complete likeness of a man. He was fair to see, big and strong, and his name was Buri. He begot a son named Bor. This son begot three sons, Odin, Wili, and Wé. These were Gods.'

'And how did the sons of Ymir agree with the sons of Bor?'

'The sons of Bor,' said Har, 'slew the Giant Ymir, and his blood drowned all his children except one called Bergelmi, who saved himself and his wife in an ark. The gods made the earth out of Ymir's body in the midst of the chasm. His flesh was the land, his bones the mountains, his blood the sea.'

Here Jafnhar spoke: 'The blood ran out of his wounds in a great ring encircling the earth. On the shore of this ocean dwell the Giants.'

'Ymir's skull,' said Thridi, 'made the heavens above the earth. They set a Dwarf at each of the four quarters, North, South, East, West. With the sparks and flakes of fire scattered from Muspellheim they made stars to move in the heavens, to give light, and to mark the days and nights, spring and summer, autumn and winter.'

'Do the Giants not seek revenge?'

'They are kept out by a great wall,' said Har. 'Inside this wall is Midgard, the abode of men.'

'But where did men come from to dwell in Midgard?'

'As they were walking on the sea-shore, these sons of Bor found two trees, and taking them up made them into men. Odin gave them breath and life, Wili gave them the power to know and to move, Wé gave them speech, hearing, and sight. They gave them also clothes and names. The man was called Ash and the woman Elma, and these two were the first parents of all mankind living in Midgard. Then the Gods made an earthly city for themselves called Asgard, in the centre of Midgard but high above the homes of men. Highest of all in Asgard is the solitary seat of Odin, called Lidskialf. From there he can see all the world and all that men are doing therein. One of Odin's names is King of Lidskialf. Odin and Frigga, his wife, are parents of all the Gods. Rightly, therefore, is Odin named All-Father.'

For a little time Gangler was silent. Then suddenly he asked: 'What is Night?'

'Night,' said Har, 'is a Giant's daughter, and like all of them she is dark. She married one of the Gods, and they had a son whose name was Day. This child was as bright and beautiful as his father. Odin took him and his mother Night, and gave them two chariots and two horses, and gave them the heavens to drive in, first one and then the other. Night's horse is Rimfaxi; when he has run his course he stands still, champing the bit; his mouth is covered with foam and this falls to the earth, where men call it dew. Skinfaxi is Day's horse, and as he runs light is shaken out of his mane over earth and the heavens.'

'And who guides the sun and the moon?'

'Once there was a man who had two children so beautiful that he called them Sun and Moon. This angered the Gods, and they snatched up the two children and set them in the cars of the sun and moon to guide them across the sky for ever – until Ragnarok.'

Gangler had never heard the word Ragnarok. If he thought at all about it, he supposed it was only a muttering, an oath of some sort, in the throat of Har. 'Why,' he asked, 'does the sun always go on? It is as if she were flying in fear from some one.'

'She is in fear. Some one is pursuing her, and he is not far behind.'

'Who is it?'

'A wolf named Skoll, and one day he will catch her and devour her. Another one named Hati follows the moon and one day will devour him. They are two of the children of the old giantess living in Iron Wood on the east of Midgard. She has many children.'

Gangler thought for a little while of Iron Wood, and an old Giantess with a beard there in the darkness, and a herd of her children who were wolves, some of them running out from under the trees of Iron Wood to look at Midgard. Gangler had never seen Iron Wood, but when Har spoke of it he saw clearly the edge of a great wood. He was hunting a bear, and had left all his companions far behind; and it was the end of a winter's day. The bear had gone into that wood, and though he was not afraid yet he stood still, leaning upon his spear and looking at the wood. The trees were oak-trees, twisted, bare and black, and he could not see far into the wood. All was black except one tiny blot of orange on a low branch of one oak-tree. All was silent except one tiny song which came from that blot of orange. It was a robin singing, and he stood watching it. Nothing was moving inside the wood. Suddenly the light was gone, and the robin turned, flitted, and was silent. He watched for it, but in vain. Long after he had ceased to expect the bird or the song, he remained standing still with his eyes towards the forest of black oaks. It was useless now to follow the bear. Slowly he turned back and wearily retraced his steps, so that not until the night was half gone did he enter his house. Several times afterwards he turned the hunt that way in the hope of finding the forest and going into it. But he never could. Years went by, and he forgot the forest. Now he remembered it, and shuddered at the thought of the old Giantess and her wolf children that would some day devour the sun and the moon. It seemed to him that the oak forest where the bear had disappeared was Iron Wood.

ONE SWALLOW DOESN'T MAKE A SUMMER

THERE was a poet in North Wales long ago named Rhys, who loved April because he loved sun, rain, and wind, separately and all together. As soon as April came he began to write poems, saying why April was better than March and May. One year, however, he cut his hand so badly in a briar bush by the river Alun that he could not write, yet he was sure that the poem which he had made in his head on the first of April was better than any he had ever written down. He had found a swallow at the edge of the river, dead, killed by a hawk. First he had cried over the swallow. Then the sun had come out, and he made the poem. He had tried hard to write it down with his left hand, using a quill from the dead swallow's wing, dipping it in the blood of his wounded right hand. But he was too impatient. The first verse looked very bad, written slowly and awkwardly with the left hand, and he threw it angrily into the water. He had made up his mind what to do.

He went to a monk, an old man, and asked him to take down the poem from his dictation, though he knew in his heart that the poem was so good that he never would forget it. The monk did as he was asked, but Rhys left the poem with him in order that it might be copied out at leisure in his best handwriting and sent to the prince.

That night Rhys was taken ill; before he had seen another swallow he was dead. His last message was that the poem should be carried to the prince.

Now, the monk hated poems, and especially those that were written in Welsh instead of in Latin. And Rhys's poem seemed to him the most foolish poem that was ever written, even in Welsh, because every verse said that the dead swallow had brought the Summer on its wings and that now, since the bird was dead, Summer could not escape from Wales. This was ridiculous, it was a lie, said the monk. Summer was not a thing, said he. Besides, he added, Summer will come to all the world, and not Wales only. Had this Swallow brought it from land to land, he asked. Moreover, he sneered, not a thousand swallows can make Summer if it is wet and cold. For this reason, and also because he hoped that he might have the poet's place of honour with the prince, the monk destroyed the poem, and wrote a very bad one of his own.

The monk's poem was contrary to Rhys's; at the end of every verse were these words: 'One swallow doesn't make a summer.' It pleased him so much that he sent it to the prince.

But the prince loved Rhys. When the monk's poem arrived he was still sorrowing for the poet's death, and the stuff changed his sorrow into anger. 'What bad verses,' he exclaimed, wishing more than ever that he had not lost his poet. The line, 'One swallow doesn't make a summer' particularly enraged him. 'Neither does one bad poem make a poet,' he cried, as he gave the manuscript to a goat to eat. The monk was disappointed. Nevertheless, whenever a swallow came in April and bad weather followed, somebody remembered the bad poem and the line: 'One swallow doesn't make a summer'; for the verse that Rhys tossed into the river was lost for ever, and there was nothing left of his poem to prove that the monk was wrong.

Birds of a Feather Flock Together

Before the winter was at an end little Bob Dumpling of Dumpling Green in Norfolk started westward to see his father, who was at Glastonbury in Somerset. A drover from Thetford was taking some cattle as far as Salisbury, and from there had to go on to Ilchester to fetch a hundred sheep. He promised to have the boy along with him as far as Warminster, where he would hand him over to the first man going to Glastonbury. So Bob took to the road with the drover. It was that green road that guides men across England into the west. The daisies of the short turf were still covered up in frost, but in among the cattle the air was like spring, because they kept away the wind and their breath was both warm and sweet. If Bob got tired, the drover, whose name was Davy, carried him. Thus it was on Davy's shoulders that the boy first saw the towns of England – Newmarket, Royston, Dunstable, Watlington, Wantage – evening after evening. In the clear hard weather men were ploughing in the Thames valley below them as they passed by. The earth was turned up in rich, dark clods like the inside of a frosted cake, and on to the furrows descended hundreds of white gulls. When Bob shouted, the birds rose up and whirled in the air like snow. Wherever the fields had been striped black by the plough there was a dappling of white gulls on the black.

The high downs on their left hand were white, but often dotted or blotched with black rooks. In the wayside thorn-bushes flitted scores of yellow-hammers as bright as flowers on the bare branches. 'Birds of a feather flock together,' said Bob. '"Tis true, lad,' said Davy, 'though I never heard it before. 'Tis poetry, too. Some people are born to make poetry. Now, I have a little lass just gone two years old, and one day she sees a sparrow hopping close to the door and says to me: "What is it?" and says I: "A little cock sparrow," and what do you think she says? Well, she says: "Sat on a sallow." A little cock sparrow sat on a sallow. That's poetry. But it isn't true. He wasn't on a sallow, and she doesn't know a sallow from an oak. But it's poetry, and so is yours:

Birds of a feather
Flock together.

I like that. Besides, 'tis true.'

So man and boy and cattle crossed over the downs and came into Salisbury. There Davy left his cattle and got drunk for the night. Bob slept in the cathedral, as Davy had told him to do, and was awakened by the clergy and the choir coming in all in white.

'Birds of a feather
Flock together,'

said Bob, staring at them from his hiding-place. Outside the cathedral, as he sat waiting for Davy, he saw the black clergy-birds flocking together here and there, just as the jackdaws did overhead on the tall spire and in the blue sky.

Davy came at last with four other drunken drovers. 'Here's Bob Dumpling, the poet,' said he to them. 'Say the poem, Bob.'

'Birds of a feather
Flock together,'

said Bob. 'True,' said one of the drovers, 'for we be all lovers of Joan's ale, and though we be not birds, yet I think the ale gives us wings to find one another.' Davy said that he had to take care of the poet, and the others went off to scatter abroad the poem in all the ale-houses.

Bob was quickly at Warminster, but two days passed before a man could be found going to Glastonbury. In these two days somebody had got ahead of him: for the first words he heard in Glastonbury were the two lines of his poem. A man was telling a story outside the George Inn. Everybody laughed at the end of it, except one, who turned away very sagely, saying:

'Birds of a feather
Flock together.'

Bob met his father safely and in due time returned to Norfolk, but though he lived to be ninety-three he never made another poem; and so many people made out it was theirs, or nobody's, that neither he himself, nor Davy the drover, was believed, when they said that he was the author; and he was buried in a grave without a stone, nobody knows where.